Frozen Echoes

Ed Downes

Undertaker Books

UNDERTAKER BOOKS
www.undertakerbooks.com

Praise for Frozen Echos

"Frozen Echoes is a book that is impressive in both depth and scope. The characters are fully realized, down to earth, and perfectly offset by a vast and all consuming terror. Fans of cold, atmospheric, and cosmic horror are not going to want to miss this one."
-*Cat Voleur, author of* Revenge Arc

"Frozen Echoes inspires all the wide-eyed wonder and thrills of Michel Crichton at his best. This book has it all–cursed objects, political intrigue, haunted shipwrecks. An old school adventure with a dash of horror that'll entertain anyone with a pulse."
-*Caleb Jones, author of* Red Hill Paradise

"Frozen Echoes is what you'd get if James Rollins and Michael Crichton wrote a book together. Fast-paced cosmic Sci-fi horror on a huge scale. You will fly through this book—just make sure you bundle up, it's cold out there!"
-*Joe Scipione, author of* Mr. Nightmare *and* The Gods Among Them.

"Frozen Echoes is a remarkable story where Ed Downes masterfully blends multiple genres with a skill few authors can match."
-*Bram Stoker Award-winner Michael Knost*

ED DOWNES

ED DOWNES

For Mom.

FROZEN ECHOES

CHAPTER 1

Dr. Flint Hill winced as he peeled the thin black glove liners off his shaking hands. The skin underneath was so badly chapped that it bled and stuck to the fleece, and removing the gloves reopened his wounds. But there was no avoiding it. His arthritis had gotten to the point where he could barely operate the weather station dials wearing gloves. Sometimes he couldn't operate them at all and had to swallow his pride and radio for one of the bright-eyed grad students who infested the station to climb into the crow's nest to help him.

His hands were bad enough that any time he saw Dr. Julie Milroy, she'd inquire about when he planned to retire. It was a humiliating ritual, but Flint put up with it nonetheless. His plans for retirement involved dying with his fingers frozen to his research equipment somewhere out on the shelf. If he died out there, his body would stick around for a while, an everlasting meat popsicle. Like a monument. Grad students could drink schnapps around his corpse.

Flint wiggled his fingers and gasped in pain. Maybe he would break his promise to himself and talk to Bill, an old-timer mechanic with hands so calloused that Flint had never seen him wear a pair of gloves. Bill kept a tub of rank salve in his pocket. He enjoyed announcing it was made from illegal whale blubber, and applied it generously to his hands whenever he was around bright-eyed marine biologists. Flint didn't think it was actually whale blubber. Or at least he hoped it wasn't, because he was about to beg a few ounces off the old engine wizard.

As Flint waited in the crow's nest, he clicked the walkie-talkie. No sound, batteries dead. A recharge would have to wait until he was back on the station.

There was no way his fingers would be able to maneuver AA batteries out of their little cellophane package.

To take his mind off the pain, he looked out the window. The horizon cut cleanly between the blue sky and white ice. According to the temperature gauge, it was zero degrees outside. Practically tropical.

Except for his joint problems, Flint loved the cold. He believed ice and hardship were the world's most powerful tools for cutting through bullshit.

Flint worked his numb digits through his warming routine of rubbing, wiggling, and blowing, priming the blood until pins and needles indicated circulation. When his fingers were about as good as they were going to get, Flint got to work adjusting knobs and sliders and cursed under his breath in increasingly colorful language. After a moment, he realized the usually impeccable silence between these curses contained a new noise: helicopter blades. He squinted, and there it was, a buzzing black dot polluting his sky and ice, flying South so fast that if it didn't slow down soon, it would be flying North again. Must be the new grad students. Flint shrugged and got back to work. Still, as he finished adjusting the weather station, an uneasy feeling hardened like clotting blood in the pit of his stomach.

THE CROP OF IDEALISTIC, hardworking young people was larger than normal this year. Well, who could blame them? The kids were probably trying to see snow while they still had the chance. He found them in the mess hall, arguing about the most efficient way to stack supplies. A thoughtful young woman nursing a cup of the station's perpetual carafe of cocoa was trying to talk a gigantic young man out of his enthusiasm for Tetris-like perfection.

"If you do it that way, we'll have to re-stack everything every time we need one of the big boxes," she said, as if to a dense Great Dane. The young man growled, but her glare won over the rest of the students, and she directed the operation without moving off her bench. Flint sat down next to her.

"Could I talk you into bringing an old timer a cup of coffee?" he said. As she sucked in her breath to object to this possibly sexist demand, he held up his oozing hands. She switched a flash of revulsion into something a touch more compassionate.

"Arthritis," Flint explained. "I doubt I'll be able to get them around a mug for another six or seven minutes." She slid off her bench, and soon they were drinking their hot beverages together. She'd been kind enough to bring him a straw while his hands warmed up.

"What team are you on?" He'd warmed up enough for small talk.

"Geomicrobiology. I'm Suri."

"I'm Flint." He smiled at her, then lowered his voice conspiratorially. "Here's a piping hot tip. You can endear yourself to just about anyone on the station by bringing them hot coffee, but it's especially true for Doctor Kaneka. And you'll earn bonus points for calling her Doctor Kaneka, even though she'll tell you to call her June. Her dissertation committee dragged her through the mud a few too many times, and she likes to be reminded it was worth it."

Suri drank the knowledge in with her cocoa, then realization dawned.

"Flint...as in, Doctor Flint Hill?" she asked, a change in posture, wide eyes and smile giving her away her adoration. "You look different on books."

"At your service," Flint said. "Though you really can call me Flint. And, those pictures were taken a lifetime ago."

"I referenced some of your work in my application for the Antarctica program!"

"Really? Do tell." He hadn't foreseen his research having a significant impact outside of geology.

Suri explained her previous research focused on copper-eating microbes and how she had used some of his big-picture stratigraphy to identify locations where similar bacteria might be found in the Southern hemisphere. Other young people joined them as they chatted, and the conversation became loud and slightly rowdy. Flint felt a stab of nostalgia for his first time on the ice. Some of these kids would fall in love, often with each other. But once in a while, one of them would fall hard for Antarctica itself. It was too early to tell, but he would have to keep an eye on Suri. She might be one of the people who found her home here.

Around six o'clock, everyone who wasn't actively fending off a catastrophe trickled into the mess hall. Flint forced down a wave of anxiety as he made his way to the front of the room. He hadn't chosen a career in one of the most remote places on Earth because he loved crowds. But there was no avoiding it. He'd made it through several decades of Antarctica winters. He could make it through one little speech.

"Excuse me, everyone?"

A few people near him listened up, but mostly no one could hear him. He cleared his throat ineffectually for a moment before his eyes landed on Bill in the corner of the room. Bill was an absolute mountain of a man, with dexterous hands equally capable of delivering a baby or pulling a one-ton snowmobile off a man's leg. Flint had seen Bill do both, his eyes glaring out from behind a beard that could only be described as chaotic. He gave Bill a pleading look, and the big man chuckled before putting his fingers in his mouth and whistling so loudly he raised the air pressure in the room. Flint seized advantage of the silence.

"Hello, everyone. I'm not a loud man, so I appreciate your careful attention. I'm Doctor Flint Hill, director of this Antarctic research station." he looked around at a sea of curious faces. "Welcome to Outpost 56E of the Antarctic research program, or as we like to call it, 'Frozen Echo'."

The part of his brain that had expected a roar of approval was offended as blank, disinterested faces stared back at him.

"What happened to Doctor Booker?" Suri shouted from the back of the room.

"Doctor Booker, unfortunately, had to leave the station last month due to a personal medical emergency."

She got drunk and dropped a half-million-dollar infrared camera in the Amundsen Sea. The ice got to a lot of people, crept under their skin, and frosted over the parts of their brains responsible for self-control and critical thinking. Sometimes, Flint suspected the people driven crazy by Antarctica were actually the sane ones. They were living somewhere impossible, relying on a delicate life-support system built by money and science. Who could blame them for drinking too much or hanging blankets over their bunk beds and having sex with whoever was available?

Flint licked his chapped lips. "We rarely get bad apples down here. You are all knowledgeable professionals, and I will do whatever I can to support your research and help you solve any problems that may arise. I love this place, I love this station, and I am pleased to be its servant. That being said, some of you are rather young and fearless. Your primary safety concern down here will always be the cold. Do not disrespect your environment. Wear your gloves. Wear your hats. Look out for each other, preferably through protective eyewear. You should all be appropriately outfitted, but if you discover you need anything, go see Bill and he will kit you out in ugly but effective cold-weather gear. Understood?"

The young people in the front took copious notes. He saw a few kids in the back joking with each other and half-heartedly paying attention. He'd have to ask Zelda to visit them later. Usually, when new people failed to take the good-cop lecture seriously, a glimpse of Zelda's noseless face diverted them back to the path of righteousness. She was a good sport about it. A lifer, like him.

Flint continued, "Our facility is a compact marvel of efficiency, designed to maximize functionality in the harsh Arctic environment. The heart of our station is this multi-purpose mess hall, which transforms from dining area to meeting space. Next door is our lab building, where vertical storage and modular benches allow for a range of equipment without sacrificing workspace."

Looking around the room, Flint made a mental note of the new faces.

"Your quarters are made up of private sleeping pods. Built-in storage and fold-out desks make these tight spaces surprisingly comfortable. But I hope you aren't claustrophobic. The station also features a small medical bay we fondly refer to as Club Med. We also have a communications center, and gym, all designed for maximum efficiency."

Flint gestured toward the airlock at the front of the hall.

"Outside, you'll find an array of sensors and research equipment, built to withstand Arctic conditions. Life here requires adaptability and cooperation..."

The door to the mess hall opened, interrupting his lecture. Flint frowned when he saw the brown-haired man striding down the center of the mess hall, tablet in hand. Jurgen, one of the station's communications officers, should have been working his shift in the radio room.

"Boss? We couldn't get you on your walkie," Jurgen said as he approached.

Flint cursed beneath his breath. He was starting to let things slide. It might be the beginning of the end. "The battery died. I lost track of time getting to know the new research assistants. Sorry, Jurgen." He felt like a hypocrite after his big lecture on respect. He couldn't let his pain get in the way of his standards. Seeing Jurgen's face, he got even more nervous.

"What is it?" Flint said.

Jurgen leaned in to whisper, "There's an issue that needs your attention." He held out the tablet that displayed a topographical map with a red blinking dot in the middle, then motioned with his head to the hallway past the mess doors.

Flint nodded, then looked to his audience. "I'm sorry, everyone. Duty calls. We'll have to continue the orientation later."

"A CHOPPER WENT DOWN three miles south of here."

"What chopper? The graduate students are here. Their chopper came in this morning."

Jurgen passed the tablet to Flint. "I know. I... It's weird, boss. A different chopper that wasn't on the schedule. Lori didn't know about it. I thought you might. I assumed it was–"

"What?" Flint studied the blinking red map pin.

"I don't know," Jurgen said. "Maybe a medical emergency. But it was weird. We picked them up on our instruments, but they wouldn't return our calls. Then we got a single Mayday. And then we lost all communication. No radio signal. If they'd flown back north, we would have seen them leave. But instead, they just...stopped. I was about to leave to get you when we picked up something on the radio."

"A distress call?"

"Not exactly. Or, not that we know of yet. It wasn't plain language. It was a bunch of clicking noises, like Morse code."

Bill had joined them, hulking and frowning with his usual gloom.

"You speak Morse?"

Bill shook his head. "No, but this place is lousy with Boy Scouts. I'll find someone."

The old mechanic joined the mess hall crowd, approaching anyone who looked like they might have had a Cracker Jack decoder ring back in high school. Flint turned back to Jurgen.

"You get a location?" Flint asked.

Jurgen shrugged. "I can tell you where their signal disappeared. My guess is that's where they are now."

Flint pulled out his radio. "You go back to the communication center. I'll find some batteries and call you for the coordinates."

Jurgen trotted out of the mess hall while Flint headed to the clinic.

THE RESEARCH STATION'S MEDICAL facilities were tiny. Not to save on space, which Antarctica had plenty of, but to save on fuel. The little room was heated twenty degrees higher than the rest of the station, so everyone called it Club Med. Whenever Flint saw someone getting burnt out on the cold—or, more appropriately, *frozen* out—he sent them to Dr. Milroy for a checkup. The doctor maintained an array of homegrown flowers that kept the room fresh and inviting.

She always looked so alarmed when his infrequent visits, which only happened when there was a serious problem, brought him through her door, that he flushed in embarrassment. *My hands aren't that bad. Yet.*

"Relax, Doc. I'm fine," Flint said. She did relax, which lowered the tension in the room by a small degree. "How would you feel about a little field trip?"

He explained the situation with the helicopter. She looked as shocked as he felt.

"Who would fly a chopper down here without telling us?" Milroy shivered despite the relative warmth of the clinic.

Flint could hear the implication in the edge of her voice. Whoever was on that aircraft might be dangerous.

"You don't have to go," he said. Now *she* looked offended, like he'd asked her to shoot a penguin.

"Of course, I'll go. I just mean we should approach with caution. You're not going, are you?"

"No, but I'll send you with my favorite pair of binoculars," Flint said, then paused in the doorway as he moved to leave. "I gave the kids my best dress-for-the-cold speech today. I trust you'll set an example for them. I know you don't get much fresh air in here."

He could practically hear her eyes roll.

A few minutes later, Flint had his rescue team assembled. Dr. Milroy, Bill, and his senior research tech, Federico, who spent his vacations chasing various cold weather extreme sports around the world and had powerful brawny thighs that made pants shopping a challenge. There was a nagging fear in the bottom of Flint's stomach, so he decided to send them with the only firearm at the station, a well-maintained Sig Sauer P320 9mm that had never been needed until now.

You couldn't shoot the weather.

Flint's anxiety was eased by the fact that Bill kept an enormous hunting knife strapped to his belt, which he used for everything from cleaning his fingernails to spreading Nutella on toast.

"I'd come along, but, uh..."

"Can't let the inmates run the asylum," Bill said.

"Sure. Something like that." Flint was about to ask Bill for a little of his whale grease, but the hulking man was already gone, striding toward the snowmobile bay with careful efficiency.

CHAPTER 2

FLINT STARED AT THE unconscious men in the clinic. Normally, the little room only had one exam table, and they'd had to dig up a second one from their emergency supplies in storage. Bill was in a chair in the corner, snoring softly, water dripping from the melted snow in his beard. He had searched the injured pilots for weapons when they'd arrived at the station and had come up with quite the little cache, which he'd locked in the pharmacy closet for lack of a better storage solution. Flint suspected Bill claimed a few items for himself.

The pilots, who were East Asian but otherwise not identifiable, had had a few bigger guns, which Bill had left on their helo. They wouldn't be returning to the wreckage without help anytime soon, and he saw no reason to add oil to the fire back here at camp. What the team had seen had impressed Bill enough that he refused to leave Dr. Milroy alone with her patients, unconscious or not. That she was spooked enough to agree to this demand alarmed Flint.

"How are they?" Flint asked.

Bill snorted and jolted awake.

Milroy was grim. "They're lucky to be alive. They both have the type of traumatic injuries you'd expect after a helo crash. Hypothermia has set in a bit, which you would also expect. I think they'll pull through, though. They're in their twenties in peak physical condition. And when I say peak, I mean Mt. Everest. I'm pretty sure whoever sent them here sent the creamiest cream of the crop."

Bill piped up from the corner. "I couldn't find a single personal item on them. Not one. Most military guys, they've got a lucky charm, a photo. These guys are outfitted like mercenaries."

"What?" said Flint.

"Actually, they're outfitted like elite government black ops troops *pretending* to be mercenaries, which worries me more."

Bill was right. The pilots had a hardened, rough-around-the-edges look that made them unlikely to be standard military. Something about their equipment and uniforms was also off, like they were too *new* to have ever seen real service. The larger pilot had a light complexion and an old, deep purple scar that ran from his scalp, over his face, to his right shoulder. The smaller pilot was covered in skull tattoos, both arms and torso.

"How many skulls?" Flint asked.

"Over a hundred, easily."

"Someone will be able to ID the helicopter," Flint said.

"Yeah." Bill sounded as uncertain about it as Flint felt.

"You think Keiko will be able to decrypt the black box?"

"Based on what we've seen so far, I doubt it. And anyway, that would just tell us why they crashed. We need to know why they were here at all." Bill glared at the nearest unconscious man. "I'm pretty sure I saw a ground penetrating radar unit in the wreck. And they had a lot of expensive camera equipment."

"Until we know more, I want Scarface and Skeletor in restraints and under guard 24/7," Flint said.

"Way ahead of you, boss." Bill was already prepared with zip ties.

Flint left the room, more confused than when he'd entered. What possible interest could the military, *any* military, have in Antarctic research? They weren't mining uranium down here.

Flint went to check on Keiko, the station's one-woman code guru. She did everything from helping research teams process their data to fixing wonky code on the sensor array that kept their produce storage rooms at a reasonably heated temperature. He still thought of those rooms as refrigerators, even though they had to be heated.

Flint found Keiko in her little den off the mess hall, cross-legged on the floor under a wool blanket, the exposed tips of her fingers poking out of the frayed cutoff ends of a pair of cashmere gloves. Flint's poor hands had been the beneficiaries of a number of pairs of Keiko's hand-knit gloves. The room was basically a closet, but there was something festive and cocoon like about it. Keiko had knitted custom covers for all the equipment that functioned better at warmer temperatures, and given her preference for jewel tones and neon accents, it was like stepping into a rainbow. She looked up as he came in and waved him over to look at her screen.

"Is this from the black box?" he asked.

"Yes. Well, sort of. 'Black box' is a little bit of a misnomer in this case, as those just contain cockpit recordings and flight data. That was all boring. They had some typical problems with ice combined with engine failure. That's common down here. The cockpit recording is just two hours of silence, a few minutes of them taking photos and talking to one another, and then the crash."

"What language were they speaking?" Flint asked.

"Chinese. Central Mandarin, I think. Official, you know, not a regional dialect. Here's what's different: In addition to the normal cockpit recordings, the black box also had some data storage capacity, which isn't typical. Most of it is encrypted, but I managed to skim a few raw image files off the top."

Flint peered at her screen.

It took a minute for his brain to connect with what he was seeing. Some of the images were familiar, the same rocks and ice he looked at every day. But the thing sticking out of the ice was...

"That's a *ship*," he said. And not one of the modern research vessels that carried supplies around this part of the world. This was a wooden sailing ship, its lines conjuring images of Barbary pirates.

"Where was this taken?" he asked.

After a long pause, Keiko shrugged and pointed in the general direction of the South Pole. Her message was clear. *Somewhere out on the ice.*

"It looks old," Flint said.

Keiko looked up. Her eyes conveyed agreement, and she went back to staring at her screen.

Flint let out a deep huff. It took him a moment to realize he'd balled his hands into stiff fists. He held his breath and slowly unfolded his fingers, feeling the joints crack as painful shocks ran up both of his arms.

CHAPTER 3

DR. EVA WARD HAD heard people call the Amazon the lungs of the planet, but to her, it looked like a hairy green armpit—and she was pissed she was about to die there.

First of all, Rodrigo, her discount bush pilot, refused to use navigation software. Fine. She doubted any government was interested in the man's small-scale smuggling of tropical hallucinogens, and at the end of the day, it was his plane.

But if a third-world bush pilot was going to forgo traditional navigation, he should at least have the decency not to hold his map upside-down. Now they were thirty miles off course with twenty miles of fuel left, in a tin can with wings that wasn't a glider. The plane bucked, and Eva's stomach dropped to somewhere near her toes.

Growing up, she thought she liked antiquities. But it turned out what she liked was museums. Air-conditioned museums with good lighting and imposing multimillion-dollar endowments. The auction houses were okay, too. Especially the high-end ones, with the velvet seats and the gilded paddles, and anonymous billionaires calling in large bids over landlines so ancient they could have been auctioned off as the last items of the night.

What Eva had discovered, to devastating effect, was that antiques were just stuff that had belonged to people as stupid as all the people alive today. With the major difference being *historical* people had lived, almost by definition, in cramped houses with no air conditioning at all.

She hated fieldwork. She hated fields in general, unless someone had already set up a luxury tent in them—and even then, they were on thin ice with her.

The pilot could land the plane in the middle of the mighty Amazon River, letting them take their chances with the pink river dolphins. But he seemed allergic to the idea of continuing to live without his plane, and so he had turned into the jungle.

"Why are we climbing?" Eva said.

Rodrigo touched the little medal of St. Joseph of Cupertino on the dashboard and murmured a prayer under his breath.

"We'll be able to glide longer without fuel from higher up," he explained without looking at her.

Eva closed her eyes, trying to think nice thoughts, then decided she didn't want to spend her last minutes staring at the back of her own eyelids. She opened her eyes again and regretted that, too, as she saw wispy clouds around her and the Amazon running like a trail of spit beneath them. Curse this stupid planet and its weakling need for oxygen.

"We're beginning our descent," Rodrigo said.

"What does that mean?" Eva shouted. There was a long pause.

"It means we've run out of fuel." Rodrico banked the plane toward the Rio Negro.

The cabin shuddered, and silence wrapped around the plane as the engines cut out. They were descending, alright. More like falling out of the sky.

The greenery beneath them crept up toward the plane. Eva hoped whatever jaguar ate her body would appreciate the nice whiskey in her stomach.

And then, out of nowhere, a gap opened up in the trees. A thin dirt line in the middle of the rainforest. She wondered how Rodrigo had managed to find it; the landscape all looked the same to her.

The runway rattled the plane, but somehow they finished the trip not only alive but upright. As he disengaged his instruments and snapped his seatbelt free, Rodrigo let out a whoop of joy that sounded more surprised than anything else. He still had his plane.

A moment later, a man poked his head out of the jungle at the side of the dirt road. When she was done taking deep breaths of relief, Eva scrambled out of the airplane.

"*Doctora* Ward?" the man asked. Eva nodded. "Bem vindo! Please follow me." He pushed aside some vegetation, and Eva saw the rusted bumper of an old black Jeep.

"You must be my driver, then." She hoped she wasn't about to regret not dying. *Hotel, museum, artifact, home.*

THE ONLY GOOD THING about the heat in the rainforest was that the "rustic" lodge's total lack of hot water didn't bother her as much as it could have. The place felt like it was designed to be as uncomfortable as possible or, as the brochure put it, "eco-conscious." Eva was already itchy and anxious, and she spent extra time trying to relax under the low-pressure, tepid stream of her room's shower. After a minute, she gave up on the idea of enjoying herself and put on a matching shirt and trousers. She hated people who took pride in putting function over form, but she was forced to admit snow-white linen might not have been the best choice for this particular adventure. It was time to brave dinner.

Like everything else in the resort, the bar looked as if it had been built from Lincoln Logs and spit, but it was shaded, and it had a terrific view that stretched out over the silvery landscape of the Rio Negro running alongside it. Being this close to the water cooled things down considerably, she admitted.

Taking a seat at the bar, Eva eyed the unlabeled bottles behind it with grim determination. The bartender, a young Kayapo woman who looked barely out of her teens, smiled.

"Do you have a wine list?" Eva asked. An obnoxious snort echoed from the darkest corner of the bar. Following the sound to its source, she saw a disheveled man outfitted head to toe in beige smirking at her.

"They've got a great *Chateau Lafite,*" he said.

"Perhaps you would like a bottle of Dom Perignon?" the young bartender asked, pronouncing the words carefully.

Eva narrowed her eyes. "Do you actually have either of those things?"

"No!" the young woman said.

"Then give me a glass of whatever you have that's most likely to burn if set on fire."

The bartender smiled and poured a generous three fingers of a milky orange liquid into a dented tin mug. Eva took a cautious sip and felt the roof of her mouth burn.

"This will do nicely," she said, before slugging the concoction and asking for another.

Mr. REI, who appeared to be drinking the same corrosive orange liquid, picked up his glass and moved to the bar stool beside her.

"I'm Xander. You can call me Xan."

Eva shook his hand. "You can call me Doctor Ward."

"Medical doctor? Dentist with a complex? Poetry dissertation?" He said the last one with a slight smirk.

"I'm an archaeologist," she said. "What about you? What do you do when you're not clearing out the local mountaineering outfitter's bargain bin?"

Glancing down at his vest, the man looked wounded. "I'm a journalist."

"You're awfully far away from a city with enough Ramen noodles and studio apartments to support a journalist," Eva said, trying not to let any of the blinding orange liquor drip onto her white pants.

"Yeah, yeah. I get it. I should introduce you to my mother. You can join her in her endless campaign to convince me to go to law school."

Eva rolled her eyes. "Law school is for people without enough imagination to get rich doing something interesting."

Xander brightened. "That's right. Although I don't care much about being rich."

"I can see that," Eva said, then felt ridiculous. As if she was one to talk. But the insult appeared to slide over him like a canoe over dark waters.

Pretty soon, they were eating piranha over mashed taro together. The bartender, Maria, who was home helping her parents for the summer between semesters at the University of Manaus, was eager to practice her English with someone other than Xander, and soon Eva learned Maria's life's story, including too much information about a boyfriend in Manaus and a botany post-doc from Ethiopia. The sunset glittered across the water outside the window, and as the conversation got rowdy, Eva struggled to put her finger on the emotion she was feeling.

Is cheap liquor in a cheap hotel making me happy? O, how the mighty have fallen.

She tried and failed to convince Maria to pour her another drink, then excused herself to go collapse in her room. Xander, looking glassy eyed himself, watched her leave.

"Sleep tight, Doctor. Good luck keeping those pants clean!"

She smirked and took a last look at the gloomy expanse of darkness outside the window of the lodge. It was the loudest quiet place she'd ever been. Insects chittered, and monkeys howled. She could practically hear the trees growing.

What had she gotten herself into?

THE NEXT MORNING, EVA was awakened by an earsplitting knock at her door. It had the acoustic quality of someone cracking a skull open with a green coconut. She threw on a shirt and found Maria standing outside with a steaming mug. The young woman thrust it into Eva's hands.

"The men at the bar were insistent I wake you. They seem unhappy. I brought you coffee. I grew the beans myself."

"What time is it?" Eva had had the foresight to set her alarm early into last night's drinking, and plugged it in to charge before passing out. As she padded back over to her bed, feeling guilty about inhaling what was some of the best coffee she'd ever had, she saw her phone was dead.

"We lost power last night for four or five hours," Maria explained.

Eva muttered a colorful curse under her breath at a low enough volume she hoped Maria wouldn't ask her to explain it.

"Tell them if I can fly into a malarial swamp, they can wait another five minutes."

Maria frowned. "There is little malaria here. The mineral content of the Rio Negro kills the mosquito eggs."

Eva shut the door in the young woman's face. Then paused, reconsidered, and reopened the door.

"Bring more coffee!" she said.

Eva squinted against the light streaming through her window. The vegetation, which had seemed lush and mysterious yesterday, looked sweaty and oppressive under the morning sunlight. She had a vision of sitting down to rest on a stump and being overtaken by parasitic vines that squeezed the breath from her lungs. If she stopped moving, this place would decompose her. She shivered and threw on another cotton top, less snowy and more eggshell.

THE MEN WHO MET her downstairs pushed their coffees to the side before she was halfway in the room, springing to their feet.

"We will go to the museum now," one of them announced. He was tall, thin, and fidgety. The undersides of his nails were filthy with dirt, and his calluses screamed "fieldwork." Ugh.

Eva rolled her eyes and picked up the second cup of coffee Maria pushed toward her. She sipped it slowly, out of a sense of spite.

"Please, Doctora," the other man said. He was a head shorter than her, with a muscular build and the annoying air of someone whose authority came from unadulterated competence. He introduced himself as Dr. Armand Martin, the man she'd been corresponding with about an unusual artifact uncovered in the middle of the rainforest. Eva was about to take another reproachful sip of her coffee when she saw a glint of emotion in the man's eyes. He wasn't annoyed, she realized. He was anxious and perhaps a little afraid. Well. The museum had paid her an irrational amount of money to fly down here. She could forgo the rest of Maria's excellent coffee.

THE BOA VISTA REGIONAL museum was a small building, equally divided between natural history and Kayapo culture. It was well curated despite its size, with a prominent reputation in the antiquities community.

The men who had met her at the lodge were the chief curator and his assistant, who represented two-thirds of the museum's staff. The building's third employee was a sullen teenage boy who glared at Eva when she walked in the door, declining to take off his headphones. Eva, who treated all museum patrons as guilty until proven innocent, winked at the teenager with silent approval.

"That is my son," said Dr. Martin. "Someday, I will send him to your country to be with the people of his heart. He is a... I think the word is *goth*?"

A snort forced its way up Eva's nose, which she tried to cover with an unconvincing cough.

"You've hustled me here," Eva said. "May I see the artifact now?"

The museum had an underfunded but spotless lab, and Dr. Martin led her to the bench in the middle. There was a nondescript plastic tub sitting on the bench, and Dr. Martin popped open the lid. As he laid it beside the plastic tub, Eva looked inside the container. The huge amount of trouble it had taken her to get here had piqued her interest. Dr. Martin stepped aside to allow her to look in the box.

A shiver ran up her spine. The object inside was a cylinder made of bone, about ten inches long, punctured with holes in a complicated pattern, like a wooden recorder on Ayahuasca.

A bone flute.

"You found this in a burial mound?" she said. "Where, exactly?"

Dr. Martin pulled out a paper map of the area, on which he'd made careful notes of his archaeological dig sites. He pointed to a mark about ten miles north of a nearby bend in the river.

"Here," he said.

"What do you know about the material?" Eva asked.

"Not much. We decided not to do destructive testing until you'd had a chance to look at it," Dr. Martin said. "We're not even sure it's bone."

Eva stared at the artifact in silence for a few seconds. It certainly captured attention. "I'd like to run some tests, take the flute with me to Sao Paulo. They have an excellent lab."

Dr. Martin looked at his assistant, worry creasing his brow. There was a long silence, followed by a furious conversation in what was neither English nor Portuguese. Eva assumed it was Kayapo. Finally, Dr. Martin put a silencing finger to his lips and turned to her.

"This may be possible," he said. "But there is something you should know."

Dr. Martin's assistant fidgeted. Eva felt the excitement in her spine dissipate into something darker and more anxious.

"There were six people working at the dig site the day we pulled the artifact out of the ground. Of those six people, five are now dead. I was working in the field tent at the time, at the farthest location from the dig. It was wrong of me. The site was my responsibility.

"Still, we have not determined the precise source of the hazard. Some of the young people had symptoms similar to those with acute radiation poisoning. I...have not been well, Doctor Ward. But my expertise is at your command for as long as it lasts."

Eva took a reflexive step away from the bone flute. Dr. Martin shook his head and tapped a 1950s-looking, toaster-sized Geiger counter sitting on a bench beside him. "The object is no more radioactive than a banana. And Augusto here has been unaffected by his time assisting me in the lab."

"I'd like to examine the dig site," Eva said.

Dr. Martin and Augusto exchanged a look.

"You must understand, Doctora. The other archaeologists who died...they were young people. Locals. There were rumors of a curse. The forest was cut down and burned."

Eva felt an involuntary hiss escape her lips. In her experience, burning things down rarely made anyone safer.

"So you see, Doctor Ward. I am willing to part with the object. But there is a risk, and I wish you to accept it willingly. I fear I will be dead before I understand the true nature of the threat."

Eva stepped once again toward the flute. *It's wrong to think of it as a flute. You're making assumptions. It could be a drumstick, a shot glass, or a ceremonial cure for radiation sickness.* Then again, her hunches were rarely wrong. Eva remembered the story of the Pied Piper of Hamelin, who had lured rats and then children out of a village with a magic flute. *If I played this flute, would I lure something, or would I be lured?* She stared at Dr. Martin.

"Pack it up. I'll go to Sao Paulo."

CHAPTER 4

"I want to go to that ship," Flint said, crossing his arms.

Bill grinned. "Aye, aye, Cap'n. But I think whoever goes to loot it should get an equal share of the treasure."

"We're not looters. I want to know why there was a spy plane taking photos of her."

"Her?" Julie said, rolling her eyes.

"Ships are women. I don't make the rules," Flint said.

"If you're such a boat expert, how come we don't know anything about this thing's age or country of origin?" Julie said.

That's why Flint wanted to go look at it. To be honest, he would want to go check it out even if there wasn't clandestine international interest. He might be a dyed-in-the-wool rock nerd, but it wasn't every day he got the chance to investigate a frozen wooden ship.

Bill cleared his throat. "When I was a kid, I had a ship in a bottle from Hamburg, Germany. It came with a little pamphlet that said it was a 17th-century frigate. That thing in the ice looks a little like that ship."

Julie had been on the station long enough not to underestimate Bill, but she still looked skeptical. Well, Flint felt plenty skeptical himself.

Julie stood up straighter than usual.

"We're hard scientists. We're not...people science experts," she said.

Flint chuckled. "People science? You mean, what? Archaeology? Anthropology? Antiquities?"

"That's what I'm talking about. I don't even have a grasp of the basic vocabulary. Would you let an anthropologist march around with one of your ice core samples?"

Flint sucked his teeth in horror. She had a point. They weren't the dream team. Still, he had a compelling desire for more information.

"Would either of you care to take on the fuck-ton of paperwork it takes to run this place?" Flint asked. Julie shook her head. Bill nearly ran out of the room. "Well then. I'm in charge. So, I'm assembling a team. We're gonna go poke around that ship."

Julie shrugged. Bill grinned. Flint made his way to the electronics lab to see if his drone was ready.

CHAPTER 5

As Eva's ride-share turned toward the University of Sao Paulo, a sickening déjà vu washed over her. The last time she'd had this feeling—of sitting on a colossal and career-changing discovery—she'd gotten screwed. *Professor Wulf.* Even the thought of his name jabbed a spear into her heart. Well. Unless he had gotten a transfer across the Atlantic Ocean, he wasn't likely to scoop her here. The department at USP was new, enthusiastic, and scrupulously ethical. So scrupulous, in fact, she might have to tell them about the bone flute's curse. She sighed and looked at the low smog over the campus buildings. She would pipe her pied way across that bridge when she got to it.

Her anxiety faded in the lab's powerful air conditioning. It was the middle of the summer in Brazil, but she may as well have been on the South Pole. *I should have brought more cashmere.*

Six hours later, she was at a small desk a cheerful admin assistant had drummed up for her, staring at an instrument readout on her laptop. After opening and closing her jaw a few times, she picked up her phone and dialed Dr. Martin. He answered on the third ring, then spent a full twenty seconds coughing, then apologized profusely. She dismissed his apology and told him she was emailing him a document. A few minutes later, she heard some typing, then an amazed silence.

"Our flute is old. Really old. Radiocarbon dating confirms it." Dr. Martin coughed a little more. He had the decency not to question her research techniques, at least. "I am not sure how this is possible. How could the flute be fifty thousand years old? Human civilization on this continent only dates back eleven thousand years."

"Actually, it's more like twelve. But you're right, it's impossible. I don't know," Eva said. "But the science doesn't lie. Maybe the people who hoofed it over the Bering Strait brought it with them."

"Perhaps," Dr. Martin said, sounding skeptical.

After they hung up, she spent several more minutes staring at the pattern of holes drilled in the flute. They had a mesmeric quality; staring at them was like falling into a spiral.

Eva's phone interrupted her reverie, a loud blare that made her teeth clench. The ringtone was one she hadn't heard in years. But there it was: the opening bars of "O Fortuna." She'd picked the sound as a joke back in grad school when hearing from Dr. Sigmund Wulf was a surefire sign of the apocalypse.

"Are you alright?" a lab assistant asked her.

Eva shook her head, realizing she was staring at the phone like it was a venomous snake. She turned off the ringer and put it into her pocket. More déjà vu.

"I'm fine," Eva said. "Never trust your advisors. Not until you see your name in *Nature*. Got it?"

The young woman smiled. "I *was* in it last year. Corresponding author!"

Eva smiled at the girl's optimism. She recognized the expression. She'd worn it often before Sigmund Wulf, supreme asshole, had wiped it off her face forever.

The worst thing about what he'd done to her was the whole department knew. They knew it had been her research, her discovery. They knew he'd taken her name off the paper and then started a whisper campaign about academic malfeasance behind her back. Not a single viper in that den had stood up for her. They had continued their probing investigations of the sand around their own heads, glad Wulf's fury hadn't landed on them.

Why would he contact me now? I'm surprised he would have the guts to remind me he's still alive.

She turned down a cheerful invitation to eat cheese bread in the student lounge and caught a car back to her hotel, with the bone flute secured in her bag.

CHAPTER 6

Flint declined the opportunity to fly the drone himself, citing the fact that he'd grown up in the pre-video-game era. "Young people these days have better dexterity," he announced, keeping his arthritis-stiffened hands in his pockets.

"Well, we'll have about one generation before AI gets faster than we possibly could be." Keiko looked down at her handheld controller, then out at the little quadcopter drone perched on a chunk of ice. It lifted into the air with a whirr.

Flint shouldn't have joined the field team. He was a liability rather than an asset in the field these days. His fingers burned with the cold, and he was beginning to worry he might not be able to hold the poles of his skis on their way back.

He shook his head to clear it. The time for regrets had passed. He was here. They'd skied out onto the ice as far as they could go. Now, a large crevasse blocked their path. The ship was frozen into a chunk of shelf ice. Flint guessed it had been buried under the snow until recently, with rising temperatures popping it out of the ice like PEZ from a dispenser.

According to Federico, accessing the ship might be possible at its current location. But it would be dangerous, with a non-negligible chance someone might get pressed flat between competing ice shelves. He'd recommended checking the site out by drone first.

So here they were. Flint resisted the urge to look over Keiko's shoulder, though he doubted the young woman would notice. She was concentrating hard, the tip of her tongue sticking out of the corner of her mouth.

"You're recording, right? You pressed the on button or whatever?" There was enough certainty in Keiko's subsequent "uh-huh" for Flint to feel assured she'd heard the question.

"Okay. I can see the mast. I'm flying down the side of the ship. The condition is incredible. Praise the ice gods for martinis and ancient ships."

"Can you see any identifying information?" Flint said. There was a long pause before Keiko answered.

"They didn't exactly paint cute names on the sides of 18th-century sailing vessels. But the masthead..."

Keiko sounded uncertain. Flint let the young woman's words hang in a claustrophobic silence. It was a trick he'd learned from his own supervisor way back in the Paleolithic era.

Keiko broke the silence with a cough. "You know how we all play *Bonny Seas?*"

Last winter, the massive multiplayer online game had gone through the station like wildfire. It was set on an ocean planet, and from what Flint knew, you sailed around in historic ships making alliances, rafting up, and fighting naval battles. The game had been so popular Flint might have tried it if it weren't for his hands. *What the hell does this game have to do with our ship?*

"The ships you can collect are all real ships, you know? One time I took down the *Lusitania* with the *Nina* and the *Santa Maria*. I didn't even have the *Pinta,* and I still managed it."

Flint rolled his eyes but decided to let the kid finish her story in her own time.

"Anyway, last year there was a big winter event. In-game. For Christmas, or Hanukkah, or whatever. And there was this one ship, this legendary ghost ship from the 1760s, everyone wanted to get. I had to spend ALL my free time harvesting ambergris so I could get it. The ship was called the *Bethany Rose.* It was transparent because it was a ghost ship. That's why everyone wanted it. And it had this really distinctive masthead of a mermaid with her eyes gouged out and a raven sitting on her head."

Flint, who had more or less had enough, cut in. "So what? The ship was from the same era or something?"

Keiko moved toward Flint, not taking her eyes off the drone's view screen. Flint looked down at the screen. On the small display, clear as whiskey ice, was a mermaid with bleeding eyes and a raven on her head. You could even still see a little of the black paint that had once covered her hair.

"So, this was a real ship?" Flint said. "What was she built for? Hell, what flag was she flying?"

Keiko cringed. "All the ships have little historical descriptions in the game encyclopedia. I didn't read any of that, though. I just thought the clear ship looked cool."

Now he'd never be able to convince these young people their games were a waste of time. It was just as well. They'd only ask him how he'd spent his downtime during World War I and what it was like to ride a penny-farthing bicycle.

"Can we get a look inside? Fly the drone down through the…ship holes?"

"Ship holes? Wow. You're really breaking out the nautical vocabulary. I think you mean the hatches."

"Okay. The hatches. Can we fly the drone down through the hatches?"

"They all look pretty iced over," Keiko said, sighing. "Speaking of ship holes, though. There's a big tear in the side of the ship. It looks new, maybe from when the ice moved and exposed it. We might be able to fly—"

Keiko's musings were interrupted by a crackle from the radio.

"Flint?" Dr. Milroy's voice rose from the vicinity of his hip. Urgency vibrated in her voice, and Flint wiggled his fingers. Gasped slightly from the pain. The devils were at it again, pricking his joints with hot pokers and pouring acid in the holes. He took a deep breath and swallowed his pride.

"Can you get the radio for me, Federico?" he said, looking at the young man. "My arthritis is acting up pretty fierce."

Federico looked more concerned than annoyed and flipped on the walkie-talkie, holding it up to Flint's mouth.

"Julie? Flint here. Station, okay? We're having quite the little exploratory venture."

There was a pause. Julie coughed. "Flint. The Navy is here."

The Navy? Well. He guessed someone had to come to pick up those injured pilots. Still, they'd gotten here awfully fast. What had they been doing, Falkland Islands war games in the South Atlantic?

"I'm guessing you're not talking about another cohort of *Bonny Seas* players?" he said. He heard Julie snort. He'd thought she shared his low opinion of the game until he'd found her leading a raid in Club Med, the only place in the station where his team's fingers could get warm enough to defeat something called the "Great Magellan Snake."

"It's the actual Navy, Flint. They have a big boat flying the American flag, and the station is swarming with strapping young sailors. You'd better get back here before they press-gang us."

"Roger that, Doc. We will ski like the swift Southern wind. Flint out."

SHE WAS EXAGGERATING A little, but not by much. When he returned to the station, a couple of zodiacs were making trips back and forth across the bay to a large American warship. The Navy bigwigs, not satisfied by the speed of these water taxis, had landed a helicopter on the ice.

As Flint crossed the mess to his office, he noticed an unusual gloom. There were a couple of soldiers standing among the tables, guns slung over their shoulders. The scientists who had stayed in the room had migrated toward the corners, occupying the spaces as far away from the young soldiers as possible. Flint frowned and approached one of the young men.

"This is a research station. A small one. You don't need to play GI Joe here."

"Yes, sir. The admiral is waiting for you in your office," the young man said, relaxing not a single iota. Flint guessed the guns weren't going anywhere.

As the young man had promised, Flint found the VIP occupant of the whirlybird waiting in his office. Not just in his office, in fact, but in *his* chair. Flint stared at the man, who had mousy brown hair. Flint hated military people. They all looked and thought alike, and they came with horrible amounts of paperwork.

The man in Flint's chair did, at least, stand up when Flint walked into the room, sticking his hand out and introducing himself as Rear Admiral Vernon Ash. *God dammit.*

"You'll pardon me for not returning your handshake. We just got a new batch of grad students down here with whatever germs they brought with them. I'm trying to avoid a bunch of uncommon colds."

"Can't be too careful at your age, sir," the rear admiral said, the faintest glint of a blade in his voice. *Ash. Where had he heard the name, Ash?*

"The ice doesn't forgive. No matter how old you are," Flint said. Suddenly, a memory hit him in the gut. "You're young for a rear admiral."

The comment glanced off the man's steely exterior without making a dent. Shit. *What's gotten into me today?* Flint made it a point not to insult men with easy access to warheads. Well. He might as well finish what he started.

"Thanks for keeping an old man's chair warm, Rear Admiral," he said, plopping himself down in the chair with an unapologetic speed.

The rear admiral coughed and took a few steps back.

"I guess you're here for the pilots. Doc's been keeping them warm in Club Med. I confess I didn't expect you to get here so soon. They're not conscious, though. She'll have a better idea if you can move them safely."

As Flint spoke, the look on Ash's face shifted from confused to downright alarmed. He walked to the door and shouted into the mess, calling his petty officers at a volume just above the room noise. The young soldiers trooped into Flint's already cramped office, and Ash shut the door behind them.

"Is this location secure?" Ash said.

Flint couldn't help but snort.

"I'm sure there's a penguin outside conducting binocular surveillance."

"I assume you are being sarcastic, Doctor Hill, but the situation is serious enough that I am compelled to ask if you are referring to a real threat of some kind."

First, the pilots. Then the ship. Now this. Flint sighed.

"I was being sarcastic, Rear Admiral. To be honest, I have no idea if this room is secure. My nearest enemy is six thousand miles away. She got the house in the divorce."

It was a bad joke and not even honest. He sent a silent mental apology to Susan, who would probably forgive him. Without some kind of release valve, the tension in the room was going to crawl down his throat and tie his colon into an elegant bow.

"Doctor Hill. I'd like you to meet Petty Officers Jered and Syl. You can take your hats off, boys."

The soldiers removed their helmets. Their hair underneath was perfectly cropped, and their faces were devoid of body fat. Oh, to be young again.

"Now. Tell me about these pilots."

Flint explained, going over the downed flight and the rescue mission in as much detail as he could. He decided not to say anything about the ship on the ice. Someone would tell them. His team wasn't super tight lipped. When Flint finished, Ash thanked him.

"We're going to take those pilots off your hands," Ash said. "The Navy's better positioned to take heat from the People's Republic for capturing enemy combatants."

"I wasn't planning on publishing a story of triumphant conquest in the *American Journal of Geology*," Flint said. Then he paused, a realization washing over him.

"If you didn't come for the pilots, why are you here?"

The petty officers exchanged a glance, poker faces in place. Ash took a deep breath, sat down across from Flint, and pulled a laptop out of his attaché case. He turned the screen so Flint could see a satellite image of the station and the surrounding Antarctica shelf. There was a large red area mapped out on the ice, from almost the ocean to several miles inland.

"That big angry rash on the map. Are your people doing any research in that area?"

"Probably," Flint said. "I think one of Muriel's penguin colonies is out there."

"Would her research cause anything...weird to happen?"

"Weird? Is that an official military term?"

"I'm just picking the best word for the job, Doctor Hill. So. Anything weird with the penguins? Creepy? Unusual? Might even go so far as to say spooky? Anything like that with any of your people?"

Flint had no idea what this guy was talking about. Maybe he was having a paranoid episode. Then again, things *had* been weird around here.

"No. Nothing weird. We don't even have a visiting artist this summer. Sometimes they do big installations out there. I don't really understand art. Look, if you tell me what you're talking about, I might be more helpful."

Ash tapped the big red blotch on the screen.

"We picked up an...unusual signal coming from these coordinates. Some kind of code that deteriorates with distance. I just want to confirm—you're not sending out any kind of signal from that area. Equipment readings, whatever."

"No. I'll double-check with anyone working out there, but no. Nothing like that," Flint said. He could feel two deep crevasses cut into his forehead as he stared at the red area. *Digital binary code? Surely it couldn't be coming from that old wooden ship?*

"We'll go talk to the pilots now. And we found the weapons stashed in the pharmacy," Ash said, and the three men left Flint alone with his worries.

CHAPTER 7

When Eva walked past the front desk on her way back to her room, a clerk ran after her, yelling until she slowed. Eva was exhausted, not in the mood for any bad news.

Instead, the clerk handed her a package. It was brown paper, bound in a red string like an old-fashioned Christmas present. A small amount of oily black residue oozed out of a corner of the paper, slipping beneath one of Eva's nails. She shuddered as she wiped it on the edge of the package, a sudden wave of nausea rising through her chest. She checked her phone again. She'd heard *"O Fortuna"* two more times before she'd turned off her ringer.

Six texts and three missed calls. All from Sigmund fucking Wulf. The jerk hadn't even left a voicemail.

Eva was proud to have lived a life of few regrets. Most of those regrets involved early 2000s fashion. But one of the regrets, the big one—the one that elbowed all the others out of its way—was her short-lived affair with her graduate advisor. She'd even been warned about him by some of the other graduate students, which made her downfall more humiliating.

If he was making a booty call, he was about to be disappointed and creatively insulted. But Eva doubted it was that. When she got back to her room, she sat down at her desk and stared at the package. As she unwrapped it, she discovered the grease was confined to the outer wrappings. *There to stop someone from stealing it?* Inside the brown paper was a small box, and inside that box was a thumb drive and a cheap voice recorder. A sticky note affixed to the recorder said: "Destroy after listening -M.W."

I guess he did leave a voicemail.

With some trepidation, Eva pressed play.

The message on the voice recorder was strange and unsettling. Or maybe that was just how she felt about hearing Wulf's high-pitched whine again after so many years. He sounded exhausted, which served him right. The content of the message alarmed her. He was rambling on about an artifact. He kept calling it an "object of great power!" and Eva was thrilled at the possibility he had lost his mind. She would have to listen to the whole thing again, but for the time being, she focused her attention on the recorder.

"The object. It's emitting some kind of binary code as a waveform," Wulf said, his voice rising with barely contained excitement. "Up and down and up and down and up and down. People are getting sick, E. My student's hair fell out. She had beautiful red hair."

Jesus. Some men never changed. She tried to ignore Wulf's idiocy and focus on his message.

"You have to understand the signal. Someone has to understand. Before anyone else gets sick. Please, E. You should destroy this message after you get it. It's not safe. Promise me you'll destroy this recorder. You can draw a little picture of my face on it if that helps. I'll get back in touch with you soon."

Eva didn't get much information from a second listen, so she sat at the desk, staring at the recorder for another minute or so. Answering a weird, instinctual impulse, she tucked the thumb drive into her bra, then took the voice recorder to the sink and ran it under hot water until it sizzled and died.

A loud knock at the door nearly jolted her out of her skin, and she heard a deep male voice say, "Housekeeping." A moment later, her unease spiked as she heard the plastic-on-metal swish of a keycard slipping into the lock. The door opened three inches before knocking against the bolt, which she'd closed out of habit.

"Can you come back later?" she said, trying to keep the anxiety out of her voice. The door closed, and everything was quiet for a moment.

Halfway through a deep breath, the loud crack of a muscular body hitting the door echoed through the room. Whoever was out there wasn't housekeeping, and as the door creaked beneath a second hit, her confidence in the bolt decreased to zero.

On the third hit, the cheap plywood around the bolt cracked. Her assailant would be in the room in seconds. *Shit.*

Eva ran onto the balcony and slid the glass door shut behind her. An errant broom, left out by the janitorial staff, rested against the railing. Eva jammed it into the tracks for the French door, gasping in pain as a splinter on the broom handle broke off and dug under her fingernail.

Vertigo warred with adrenaline as she looked over the railing, down at the ant-like traffic buzzing below. Jumping would be suicide. She winced as she yanked a needle of wood out from under the nail of her middle finger. The noise outside was so loud Eva barely heard the hotel room door break in. A man that looked two sizes too big for his generic hotel uniform came bounding through the wreckage of the doorway. The intruder walked toward her, picked up the cheap desk chair, and smashed it through the glass balcony doors.

So much for the broom.

The broom. She crouched down alongside the door, shielding her face as the intruder kicked out a few remaining shards from the door and barreled through. As his feet passed through the gap where the glass had been, Eva slipped the broomstick out from the tracks and held it out at knee level.

The intruder, amped on adrenaline and overshooting on momentum, tripped on the broom handle and flipped straight over the balcony railing. Eva barely caught the look of surprise on his face as he reached down to catch himself and found nothing but seven stories of smoggy air beneath his flailing hands. A moment later, screams rose up from the ground below.

Eva ran through the room and almost barreled into another person in the hallway. As she raised her broomstick in defense, the smaller Brazilian woman ducked and cowered. Eva pulled the broomstick a millimeter short of the woman's face. *Actual housekeeping.*

Eva ran back into her room and grabbed her backpack from the desk. Then, she pushed the housekeeper out of her path and continued down the hallway at a dead run.

CHAPTER 8

FLINT FELT OUTNUMBERED, WHICH was unusual in a place as sparsely populated as Antarctica. He closed the door to his small office and frowned as footsteps continued to tramp back and forth in the room outside. The soldiers had transformed the already close quarters of the research station into a veritable sardine can. *More people means more warmth,* the pragmatic part of his brain noted, but Flint shook his head. These new military people were sucking the warmth *out* of the station, hoarding it for themselves like heat dragons.

Vernon Ash knew about the Chinese pilots, and he knew Flint's team had been doing research in the area.

Ash hadn't made any attempts to physically remove the researchers. But his men had secured key station resources by waiting inside them until everyone left, then locking the doors with large metal padlocks. The biology team, mired in time-sensitive research on penguin colony behavior, had raised a huge stink about losing their snowmobiles. Ultimately, June Kaneka had marched outside in full gear and shouted to her gun-toting tail that they could shoot her if they wanted, but she was going to do the research the American government had paid for. The entire team had to walk three miles to their research site every day. Dr. Milroy, worried that exhaustion would lead to accidents, was furious. She sent Zelda to visit all of them individually. When that failed, she sent Zelda to visit the rear admiral, but she knew Ash was not going to unlock the snowmobile shed any time soon.

Pretty soon, someone would have to budge. And Flint was pretty sure the rear admiral was too stubborn to budge off an anvil that was crushing his own foot.

Ash was stationed at what he unironically called his command post, which was half of one of the long cafeteria tables in the mess hall. Flint stared at him until the rear admiral offered a few terse and unemotional words. Fury boiled through Flint so fiercely that he had to stop himself from clenching his own fists, which would cause him more pain than he could handle right now. This man, with his chain of command and access to vast resources, didn't understand anything. Didn't understand that he was killing Flint.

"You win," Flint said, his voice as flat as an ice shelf. "I need twenty minutes to assemble everyone."

It didn't take long to get everyone gathered in the mess hall. Even the stalwart penguin research team was taking a rest day. When he was finished, there were fifty men and women in the hall, from old timers like Bill down to the young graduate students. He was pretty sure that Suri, whom he'd met on her first day at the station, had fallen for the continent as hard as he had. *I should be jealous.* But he wasn't jealous. He was sad for both of them.

Flint cleared his throat and found himself choking back tears. Two deep breaths took care of those.

"Look, folks. We're shutting down. Military shit. If our government spent half as much on our climate research as they do on that big turd of a boat parked offshore, we'd all be better off. They've made their stand, now I'm making mine. Everyone who's not directly responsible for keeping this place thawed out for next year goes back to the mainland. If you have to ask if you're essential, you're probably not, but go ahead and ask anyway."

There was no outraged shouting, just a quiet sense of disappointment. They'd all been staring at the writing on the wall; it wasn't a surprise to have it read out loud to them.

A few of the grad students, who had found conditions on the station harder than they'd expected, looked relieved. Suri, however, was crying. She looked at Flint like a lover in the lowest point of a tragedy, and a few tears rolled down his own face in response. He coughed.

"I'm staying to make sure none of the GI Joes break your tools. The military has declined to loan us any of their resources, including their helicopters, so we've got a fishing boat from Argentina coming for you all tomorrow. It'll take about six days to get back to the mainland, and it's not gonna be a nice ride. If you get pukey on boats, go see the doc today and she'll talk to you about motion sickness medication options. Once again, I am sorry."

He had failed to protect them. The permanent researchers, only some of whom were fit for normal society, would have to get horrible lab jobs in places with air conditioning. The temporary researchers would lose data they were counting on for tenure or promotions. The young people would suffer the worst fate of all, ripped off the ice before they got a chance to know it.

To hell with it. Flint clenched his fists, grunted in pain, and went to find Ash.

THE REAR ADMIRAL WAS in the crow's nest, which made Flint feel even more territorial. Greater annoyance gnawed in Flint's gut as he lumbered his way up the metal ladder into the small control room and found that Ash had commandeered his favorite chair. Probably some kind of bullshit military power play.

"You can't kick us off the ice. You're ruining lives," Flint said.

Ash looked out at the white and blue landscape in front of him. It was high noon, and the shadowless landscape blazed with sunlight. "From your limited perspective, I'm sure that's true. But I have a larger and unbending mandate," Ash said. There was a certain amount of sympathy in his voice.

"Perhaps we can support your mission," Flint said, taking a deep breath. "We found a ship out on the ice."

Ash raised an eyebrow, and Flint told him the story.

"We're well equipped to research it. Could be mutually beneficial. For instance, I can tell you take pride in the men and women under your command."

"They're the best of the best," Vernon said, warmth in his voice.

"Well, so are we," Flint said. Seeing Ash's upper lip soften, Flint continued with this tactic. "Tell me, Rear Admiral Ash. Why are your people the best?"

"They're well suited to their roles, and they've had the best training in the world," Ash responded.

"Bingo. Well, guess what? The military doesn't have a monopoly on excellence, they just have better funding. We have equipment that you could commandeer. But if you do that, you'll lose access to some of the finest scientific minds in the Southern Hemisphere. We're not a road bump, Ash. We're a resource pool. Let us help you investigate the ship."

The wheels turned in Ash's brain. He looked Flint dead in the eyes.

"No."

Flint's stomach sank. He pulled a walkie-talkie from his pocket, wincing as he pulled his gloves off.

"Keiko?"

"I'm here, Doctor Hill," the walkie-talkie crackled as a shaky voice responded through the cold air.

"Can you go ahead and hover your finger over that SEND button?"

"Yes, sir," Keiko said, sounding only a little like she was about to pass out from fear.

Flint stared at Ash.

"Hover your finger?" Ash said, derision running deep through his voice. "Is that formal scientific language?"

"Good solutions aren't always high-tech. Ask Bill. So. Here's the story. If you kick us out of the station, Keiko will release video footage of the ship in the ice to Facebook, Twitter, Instagram, and all the social media sites I'm too old to know about. Which means you'll have teams of treasure hunters and bored, rich Antarctica exploration wannabees breathing down your neck for months. If Keiko is really upset—which I'm pretty sure she is, she has a long-distance boyfriend she is *not* eager to spend more time with—she might throw in a few photographs of those Chinese pilots I took in Club Med earlier. And then you can have fun with the Chinese."

Ash looked unimpressed. "I can detain you indefinitely for not cooperating with me. How would you like an extended vacation somewhere off the books?"

Flint snorted. "I'll bet you a hundred bucks if you kick me off the ice, I'll be dead in less than a year."

"Cut it with the snow king crap. You'll be dead if you die, which is exactly what I'm trying to prevent." Ash sighed. His expression didn't change, but Flint could swear he saw the lines on the man's face deepen. "You know what? Fine," the admiral said. "I accept your offer of help. Your experience in this region will be welcome up to and until it comes into conflict with my authority. Is that understood?"

Flint resisted the urge, probably acquired from watching too many war flicks, to snap to attention. He tried to slouch but only succeeded in pulling a back muscle.

"Sure. Thanks," he said, as he began to climb back down the ladder. "Don't let your dick freeze off!" he shouted back up. The clanking of his boots on the ladder's metallic rungs drowned out any reply.

CHAPTER 9

EVA LET HERSELF GET lost in the maze of downtown Sao Paulo, an endless quilt of skyscrapers. There were twenty million people in the metro area. If she had no idea where she was, neither would whoever was trying to come after her. When she'd wandered for an hour and gotten herself fully lost, she ducked into a little cafe and bought a bag of cheese bread. The fluffy manioc balls melted in her mouth as she inventoried the contents of her backpack. *The artifact.* She had her wallet. A light sweater. Her university guest access pass on a festive red and black Sao Paulo FC lanyard. The hotel keycard could go into the trash. Patting her bra, Eva was relieved to find the thumb drive from Wulf was still in there. As her fingers closed around the small rectangle, she felt immense relief. Maybe she wasn't totally screwed.

Brushing the last crumbs of cheese bread off her lap, Eva reluctantly returned to the smog and noise of the street. She was pretty sure there wasn't enough cash in her wallet to rent a hotel room, and she didn't want to risk using her credit card. She just needed a place to hide for a few hours. Idly, she began to pull on the handles of cars as she walked along the street.

It took seven blocks, but finally, a car opened. The back seat of the ancient Chevy Blazer was expansive and inviting. Relieved, Eva slipped inside. If the owner came back, well, she guessed she would have the opportunity to learn some Portuguese obscenities. But for now, she had her little pod. The backseat was clean and comfortable, and her phone had a few hours of battery life left.

When Eva checked her email, she was glad she was sitting down.

Wulf was dead.

The official email from her alma mater was obtuse. A lot of fancy language about years of service but no real content. Although she snorted at the mention of "devoted students."

The news report she found when she searched for Wulf's name was more explicit.

ANTHROPOLOGY PROFESSOR DEAD IN TRUNK OF CAR. The car was found burning in the main campus parking lot. Security, assuming the fire was some combination of student prank, protest, or celebration, had taken their sweet time putting it out. It was only when a junkyard employee found the titanium knee among the ashes in the trunk that anyone realized a human being had been inside the car. The serial number on the knee had confirmed the identity of the owner.

Eva, who had fantasized about her old advisor's violent and humiliating death since she'd left school, found herself sickened by fear that she'd caused this disaster. Had she cursed him with her hatred?

According to the news reports, the police had no suspects. Thinking of the man who had just sailed over the balcony in her hotel room, Eva decided she could think of at least one.

Sighing, Eva dialed a number on her phone. She might as well get it over with.

Her ex-husband, Steve, was unflapped when she told him she'd be out of communication for at least a few more days. But he was unflappable, sometimes to the point of irritation. The world could end and his trademark surfer smile would never leave his face. Just once, she wanted to see him angry.

Even if it was at her.

Eva took a deep breath. "Is Sophie there?" she said, trying to sound casual.

"She's at a birthday party. She promised to sneak me out a piece of cake," Steve said. "You could try her cell, but I think there was some mention of a Slip N' Slide."

"I can't pull her away from the cake and a Slip N' Slide. I'm not a monster," Eva said.

"You're not a monster," Steve confirmed. "Any specific message, or the usual?"

"The usual. Love her, miss her, can't wait for our trip."

"The Galapagos. Who doesn't love to look at very specific birds? What is it, finches?"

"And marine iguanas," Eva said.

"Got it. Everything okay down there? No, uh, poison dart frogs rubbing themselves on your tongue while you sleep or whatever?"

Eva thought about telling him the truth. But she didn't know what would be worse—hearing him rattled for the first time in her adult life or hearing him brush off the assassination attempt as a *no problemo* bump in the road.

"I'm hanging in there," she said and hung up the phone. She googled the Wulf accident again, but nothing new popped up.

The inside of the car was warm, the noise outside so dense and persistent it lulled her. She shut her eyes against the drowsy sunlight as exhaustion crept in, replacing her ebbing adrenaline.

Minutes later, she was asleep.

CHAPTER 10

WHEN FLINT HAD IMAGINED the wardroom of the U.S.S. *Taft*, he had envisioned something luxurious. Gleaming banisters and shiny diplomat-impressing wood. Once inside the ship, he was forced to admit he may have been thinking of the movie *Titanic*. Instead of chandeliers and parquet floors, he found fluorescent lighting and plastic chairs bolted down at awkward distances from the particle board conference table. Which was also bolted to the floor.

Adding Flint to the team had been more than a meaningless gesture to keep footage of the old icebreaker off the internet. Since Ash had decided not to send Flint and his team home, Flint had found himself swimming through an endless sea of meetings, where his opinions were solicited and considered.

Rear Admiral Vernon Ash was clearly competent, but his overall motives remained opaque, and that made Flint nervous. Ash had conquered the Antarctic research station. Benevolently, maybe, but he had tightened an iron grip of control around the buildings and people. Grad students who would have come to him for advice a month ago had started approaching naval officers instead.

Flint fidgeted in his plastic chair as someone handed around mugs of what turned out to be good coffee. *If an army marches on its stomach, a navy sails on its caffeination.*

"We have decent amphibious capabilities, though less experience on the ice. If you can recommend anyone to advise my people on, er..." Ash trailed off.

"Freezing boat stuff?" Flint supplied. Ash coughed.

"Extreme weather naval equipment issues. Much appreciated."

Flint decided he would send them Bill as a test. There were two kinds of scientists in Antarctica. The kind that took Bill's advice and the kind that left before finishing their projects because they were too broke or injured to continue. Even after a week of working with Ash, he wasn't convinced the rear admiral was the first kind.

"I want to increase our shore transport capabilities. How many zodiacs do we have?" Ash asked.

"About half," an intense woman responded immediately. Ash's people were attentive and well trained. Ash looked at the woman, who had an interesting and alert face. Based on the gray in her hair, he guessed she was in her late forties, although her face looked younger.

"I want to get that number up. Maybe even to a hundred percent, if that's possible, Captain Sanchez," Ash said.

"Yes, sir," the woman said.

"And keep the birds on yellow alert. If necessary, I want to be able to get to the site faster than the boats can get us there."

"Yes, sir."

Only grad students from places like Alabama ever called Flint "sir." He wondered if he should start encouraging it.

Dr. Milroy, who was slumped in her chair to a degree that would impress the sullenest of teens, coughed loudly.

"Should we be going in at all?" she asked. "Maybe the signal you're so intent on pursuing is a warning. What if we're digging straight under a DANGER sign?"

"You're an excellent physician, Doctor Milroy. I checked. Working in concert with my also-excellent team on board this ship, I trust you'll be able to address any...challenges that arise."

"Unlike the United States military, I'm not eager to practice my rusty surgery skills on healthy young bodies."

Flint winced as he heard a dozen fatigue-clad backs in the room stiffen. At the moment, his hands had molded into rigid claws, but he poked Dr. Milroy's arm with one and hoped she would understand the gesture.

"After astronauts, we're the closest thing to old-school explorers," Flint said in a low voice. "This is our chance to be Amundsen on the South Pole."

"Didn't Amundsen die?" Dr. Milroy's failed veil of a smile was on full display.

"No. That was the other team. Robert Scott."

"How do you know we're not the other team?" The usual warmth in Dr. Milroy's voice was frosted over with worry.

"Our people aren't being press-ganged. It'll be volunteer only."

Dr. Milroy's eyes narrowed. "Their lives aren't disposable either," she said, pointing in the direction of the sailors. The intense-looking woman smiled briefly, then wiped her expression flat again.

"Do you know how to ice climb?" Ash interrupted. Flint looked at him.

"It's hard to have a career in Antarctica without trying at least once," Flint replied. *Exactly once. Twenty-five years ago. Before my hands gave out.* Being surrounded by soldiers kindled some idiot masculine impulse in Flint that prevented him from volunteering this information.

"Well, brush up," Ash said. "You're joining the first team out to the ship."

CHAPTER 11

Eva napped in the car until mounting anxiety got the better of her. She couldn't stop staring at her phone, battery ready to die, wondering if whoever had come to the hotel was tracking it. She had no idea how hard it was to hack another person's phone. Maybe armed men were already watching her, waiting until she went somewhere it would be convenient to murder her.

Ten minutes into this line of thought, she exited the car and threw her phone into a nearby trash can after texting Steve a quick message that she was "going off the grid." Without her phone, she felt naked from the waist down. She could buy a new burner phone with her credit card, but wouldn't they find her just as easily that way?

Eva knew one person in Rio who could help her solve this problem.

An hour later, she was in the Pinheros district, staring at a row of luxury clothing stores. She was grungy from her post-assassination-attempt ordeal and wondered if she would even be able to make it past the door guards at any of these places. Finding a few baby wipes in her pocket, Eva cleaned off her face and smiled her brightest smile. She hoped flashing a few thousand dollars of orthodontia would buy her admission into a store where the average handbag cost twice as much as her rent.

It did.

The outside of this particular boutique was nondescript, but inside, the store was beautiful. It took a lot of restraint not to run her grubby hands over the beautiful fabrics on the racks, and Eva wished she was here on a less urgent mission.

The tall, willowy, faintly terrifying woman at the counter glared at Eva, but she didn't call the guards when Eva marched up to her.

"I'm looking for Gucci," Eva said in a low voice.

The woman's glower disappeared, and she glanced around the store.

"Do you have an invitation?" she asked.

Eva wondered if this was the first time anyone had asked her about Gucci.

There was a password. Eva racked her brain, trying to remember it. She had a few too many exotic cocktails the night Gucci had given it to her, but she remembered it was something extremely stupid. A circuit connected, and Eva grinned.

"Give me couture, or give me death."

The young woman's face lit up with pleasure. She looked excited.

"This way!" she said, leaving Eva to speed walk after her clicking stilettos.

The woman serpentined her way around clothing racks until she reached the back of the store. There, an old colonial Portuguese wardrobe was bolted against the wall, looking shabby but still chic. Throwing open the wardrobe doors, the woman pushed aside a row of expensive clothing, revealing a cover-blocked opening just large enough for a person to crawl through.

Eva opened the hatch, took off her backpack, and thrust it into the tunnel in front of her.

Great, small dark paces, just what I need.

Before she could talk herself out of it, she clambered onto her knees and crawled into the dark passage, hoping she wasn't making a terrible mistake. After a moment, the shopkeeper shut the wardrobe behind her, casting Eva into darkness.

CHAPTER 12

Flint couldn't stand the metal-on-metal screeching sound his crampons made as he crossed the wobbling aluminum ladder over the gap between the ice shelf and the ship. Perhaps this was why he'd only gone ice climbing once. Quickly enough, though, Petty Officer Syl and Federico were pulling him onto the wooden deck of the ship, which was pitched at a weird angle.

Flint stared at the ancient floorboards. "Is this safe?" he asked.

"No, sir!" Petty Officer Syl replied. He watched as Jurgen brought up the rear, picking his way over the ladder. Flint unclipped his harness and looked around.

"What do we do now?" Jurgen asked, breathing hard.

"I guess we go through their bathroom cabinets," Flint said and headed toward the captain's quarters.

He had to ask one of the young sailors to kick in the door, sending a quiet apology to the archaeologists, who would no doubt be horrified by their destructive approach to discovery.

Flint wasn't prepared for the captain's body to look as if it had frozen yesterday. He had only been face to face with a dead body once in his life. He'd been a child then, dropped off at his grandfather's house for the weekend by parents who had driven off before he made the discovery.

Flint had found his grandfather in bed, and his strongest memory of that day was a smell, a soaking foulness that had distorted the peaceful picture of an old man dying in his sleep. His grandfather had been dead a few hours, and even then, the decay was pervasive. Ever since then, Flint had thought of the human body as a machine for staving off smell.

The man at the little wooden desk in the corner of the room had died hundreds of years ago, but the cold had put a stop to the normal biological processes. Flint was grateful, but there was something off-putting about it, as well, seeing a man frozen like wholesale meat. Someone who had died a death so cold and remote the ordinary rules hadn't applied. There was no decomposition, no return of nutrients to the soil. Just rigid blue flesh with a rictus grin, locked into a horrible frozen forever.

There was a fragile, browning logbook on the desk in front of the captain. Flint picked it up, contemplated opening it, and then changed his mind, imagining the book crumbling between his fingers. Hearing a shout, he tucked it into his backpack.

Jurgen and a few of the petty officers had gone through a hatch down into the ship. Flint walked over to a set of rickety steps that plunged into the black abyss of the hold. The frozen wood creaked, and he shuddered.

A young sailor handed him a flashlight, and Flint flicked it on, trudging down the narrow stairs. The flashlight had a concentrated, powerful beam, and Flint found the bright circle of light calming, almost meditative. It was a shining ring into which he could direct his undivided focus, not having to think about the seeping darkness around it.

He found Jurgen and Syl standing in front of a wooden door, prying a board off it with a thin metal crowbar.

"It was barred from the outside," Syl said.

Flint looked at the door. He wondered if it was wise to fling open a door someone had gone to so much trouble to shut. On the other hand, anything that could attack them would have been dead for hundreds of years.

Flint helped pull the board away, and it splintered off with a crack. He tossed the wood scraps onto the ground and looked at Jurgen.

"Wanna do the honors, Doc?" Jurgen asked, not meeting his eyes. He was afraid.

Flint opened the door and shone his flashlight inside.

It was a surprisingly expansive room. There was an enormous, strange object stretching from the center of the room out into the corners. At first, he thought he was looking at some kind of rigging. Four poles extended from a mass in the center, stretching almost from one side of the ship to the other.

It didn't look like wood, though. The shape was lumpier, more organic, with what looked like fringe on the ends.

Flint approached the center of the structure. There was some kind of bulb there frosted over. Flint reached out and brushed off a fragile layer of snow.

As the beam of his flashlight hit what he'd uncovered, Flint screamed and stumbled back, his light source dropping to his side. He tripped over a plank and stupidly used his arthritic hands to break his fall; his first fearful scream was followed up by a second shout of pain. Jurgen shone his light first on Flint and then back on the structure. As he did, Flint saw what he'd uncovered for the second time.

A frozen human face stretched like chewing gum and screaming in pain.

FLINT FOUND HIMSELF BACK on the deck of the *Bethany Rose,* remembering only a panicked stumble toward the light. He felt as if his body had stepped into a different reality, and his mind was still catching up.

What had happened to the man in the hold? Torture? Had his companions gone insane and done...well, whatever this horror was? Had he been the victim of obscene postmortem taxidermy? Had some kind of violent, demented artist been at work here? Flint shuttered and felt suddenly cold, despite his engineered layers. Human violence would be a horrible but comprehensible explanation. The alternatives were inhuman and unreal. Far, far outside the realm of the known. Outside even the realm of hypotheses.

No. Not outside of that. You can test any hypothesis. At the moment, he didn't care to make any.

The body in the hold had been twice the length of an average person, but he didn't think it was much heavier. Instead, it looked like a normal person who had been sculpted in clay and then rolled out, stretched longer and thinner in all directions. The skin had been taut over elongated bones. The head had sunk into the body, diminished like the skull, and vertebrae of the neck had been leached to contribute mass to the arms and legs.

An abyssal geologic noise shivered the air. Flint snapped out of his woolgather and looked down at the wood beneath his crampons, recognizing a faint vibration.

The ice was shifting.

"Jurgen!" He screamed at the top of his lungs, leaping to his feet. As he ran towards the steps into the hold, the ground buckled beneath him, collapsing into a V-shape that dropped him a foot. He felt a splinter of wood pierce the skin just above his boot, wondering if a three-hundred-year-old ship was more or less likely to carry tetanus.

The noise had gotten so loud that when he screamed for Jurgen again, he failed to hear his own voice over the creaking ice and breaking wood.

Flint stared from the ladder that led back onto the glacier to the black abyss of the hole.

At that moment, there was a sudden pause in the glacial noise as the ice and ship settled into new positions. In that sliver of time, Flint heard Jurgen scream.

He ran toward the staircase into the hold, taking the steps two at a time. As he did, he realized he'd left his flashlight somewhere on the deck.

"Jurgen," he shouted, hoping there was a chance in hell his voice might carry.

There was another crack, and the boards above him broke, dumping layers of frost onto his head. As he pawed at his eyes, he heard a voice.

"Flint!"

He moved toward it, away from the light up top, tripping down the stairs with his hands ahead of him.

An image of the thing in the hold came to him unbidden as he reached his arms out in the dark. He felt a stabbing, irrational fear the next thing he touched would not be Jurgen, but the long-limbed monstrosity, moving its spider-like limbs through the darkness. Coming for him.

He touched something that moved and screamed, a primal, caveman noise.

"Flint!" he heard a voice say. It was Jurgen. The living flesh under his hands was transformed from something horrible to something comforting.

"My foot is caught between two boards. You'll have to rip me out."

This admission was punctuated by the loudest noise Flint had ever heard, a rumble like a waking god.

All sense of propriety aside, Flint pawed at Jurgen's body until he managed to maneuver himself under the man's arm. Bracing himself, he counted to three and pulled with every bit of energy he had left.

Jurgen's scream almost drowned out the sound of splintering wood. Flint tried to ignore the scrape of wood on bone. But the tautness in Jurgen's body disappeared as his foot came free, and soon the two of them stumbled toward the light above them. A desperate rush of adrenaline allowed Flint to haul the younger man up the steps.

The ladder that spanned the gap between them and the nearest ice shelf shuddered as the boards of the ship buckled and cracked. Flint pushed Jurgen onto the ladder, hoping there would be enough time for at least one of them to get across. Jurgen, crying in pain and crawling in fear, made it halfway across before the ice shelf bucked. Flint watched in horror as the ladder detached, tossing Jurgen's body into the gap between the shelf and ship. The ice shelf moved again, crunching against the ship with a single, tremendous noise that extinguished the last of Jurgen's screams.

The ladder was gone, but the safety line they had clipped to on their way over was still dangling loose over the side of the ship. Flint saw a red-faced Petty Officer Jered screaming and pointing at the carabiner. Flint made a mad dash toward it, forcing his burning fingers to grip the latch and clip it to his belt.

Wooden boards buckled beneath, and Flint dropped a foot.

Now what?

He looked at Petty Officer Jered, riding the bucking ice shelf like it was a bronco, mouthing words inaudible over the sounds of cracking wood and scraping ice.

JUMP.

Shit.

A crack opened up between Flint's feet. If he didn't move soon, he'd be crushed by ice. Or worse, injured and buried in some pocket crevasse, where he'd freeze to death as soon as shock kicked in. The ice shelf was now about six feet higher than the ship and slamming into the wood like a piston.

Flint ran, feeling the rope tied to his harness go taut as someone up on the ice shelf brought in the slack. His adrenaline surged as he clambered up onto the ship's railing and then out toward the ice shelf.

Something cold and hard slammed against his face as Flint hit the ice. There was a warm gush as blood flowed into his eye and then froze, blocking his vision. Flint slid down the slick surface of the ice shelf.

"Get the rope!" an authoritative voice above him shouted. The light dimmed, and Flint wondered if he was passing out, but realized it was worse than that. He had fallen into a gap between the ship and the shelf, the two surfaces moving as the ice shelf pushed closer to the ship.

He felt his movement stop as the rope at his waist caught. The ship was only a few feet away now but inching closer. Soon, they would slam together, turning him into the world's least appetizing pate.

An idea came to him. Flint braced his back against the ice and put his feet on the ship. When the ship juddered upward, he jumped with both feet.

He cleared the gap seconds before the ice shelf slammed into the ship hard enough to splinter the frozen wood. Flint turned toward the ice, putting his feet against the wall so whoever was pulling him up wouldn't have to drag him over the ice.

He passed out before he reached the top.

CHAPTER 13

POP CULTURE GIVES AN image of hackers as nerdy, unwashed, naked-mole-rat typists who lived in cluttered hovels.

Pop culture never met Gucci.

Gucci wasn't his real name, of course. Eva doubted anyone in the man's life knew his real name. Five-foot-six and nothing special to look at, he made up for it with deep knowledge of and enthusiasm for three things: coding, fashion, and interior design.

After Gucci made several million dollars doing programming of dubious legality, he opened a small fashion boutique focused on Brazilian designers. It quickly became so popular his illegal activities were almost exposed during an in-depth profile by *Brazilian Vogue*. He'd been able to bribe his way out of it, but it had been a close thing. Eva had met him while he'd been spending the summer with one of her antiquities friends. She had been in deep despair over her breakup with Wulf, and he'd needed someone to do drugs with.

The tunnel she'd had to crawl through to access Gucci's home was small, but the space beyond was enormous. Eva had seen rich people's houses before, but she had never seen anything like this.

First of all, there were no windows. Gucci was terrified of surveillance, so his whole space was just an enormous box. He made up for the lack of natural light with clever design. The ceiling was a vast expanse of UV bulbs and hanging plants, spaced so densely they obscured the ceiling. Beneath the undulating waves of plants and light, the stained concrete floors were almost covered by overlapping rugs. The place carried an earthy, sweet aroma that reminded Eva of an old cigar box.

To Eva, it felt like the only reasonable type of picnic: an expensive one that happened indoors.

When Eva had emerged from the tunnel, no one had greeted her, so she explored the space on her own until she found Gucci at what she assumed was his hacking station. It was one of many little islands located in the vast room, an Italian leather sofa engulfed in so many cables and wires the furniture looked like it was being devoured by some kind of cyberpunk octopus.

When Gucci saw her, he gasped. Not, she suspected, at her presence, but at the grimy outfit she'd been wearing for the past twenty-four hours.

"Something terrible has happened to you at a Ross Dress-for-Less!" Gucci exclaimed. At present, he was wearing what appeared to be velvet pajamas printed with loud shapes in muted jewel tones. He looked impossibly chic.

"I promise I would have dressed for this, but someone tried to kill me."

To her slight alarm, Eva started crying. It was hard to beat herself up too much for it, though. Narrow escapes from death and watching people splat themselves on concrete was exactly what crying was for.

"In that case, I am forced to forgive and possibly dress you," Gucci said, patting the only twelve square inches of the sofa not covered in computer equipment. Eva perched herself on the bare spot, and Gucci held his sleeve against her nose.

"Blow," he instructed, sounding like a midwestern grandma.

"I'm not blowing my nose on couture."

Gucci rolled his eyes. "Please. I literally own a dry cleaner."

Still, Eva shook her head. Gucci lowered his sleeve, and she relayed the events of the past week, starting with the horrible flight into the middle of the Amazon. Gucci asked many insightful questions and some less insightful ones about what people were wearing and whether she'd noticed any new textiles in the jungle.

"Can you find anything out about Wulf's death?" Eva asked.

"Yes," Gucci said. "In the meantime, why don't you take a shower, and I'll find you something to wear."

"Only if you promise not to burn my clothes again. I might need to go somewhere chiffon won't cut it."

Gucci shuddered at the thought and sent her off toward the far end of the bunker.

CHAPTER 14

Flint drifted in and out of hallucinogenic dreams where he was eating frozen pate and making love to a dark-haired woman with a raven sitting on her head. The first time he came to, it was only for long enough to understand he was in Club Med. He caught a glimpse of Bill sitting in the corner, thumbing through the captain's logs Flint had pilfered from the *Bethany Rose*. Flint barely had time to hope Bill had wiped the whale grease off his hands before inky black spots crept back over his vision.

The next time Flint woke up, he found himself face to face with Rear Admiral Ash, flanked by a red-faced, irate Dr. Milroy.

"He needs rest," she whispered. Ash stared down into Flint's face.

"Would you like to go back to sleep?" he asked.

"No," Flint said.

The rear admiral nodded.

"Jurgen is dead," Ash said flatly.

"I know," Flint said.

Ash nodded. "His contributions to this mission will not be forgotten. Not by the United States government, and not by me."

"Has someone called his mother?" Flint asked.

"I tried to call, but comms are still out. Maybe you can ask the Admiral to turn them back on," Dr. Milroy piped in, her voice catching in her throat.

"The readings he captured on the *Bethany Rose* proved to be extremely valuable. They allowed us to pinpoint the origin of the signal," Ash said. The rear admiral was trying to maintain an air of solemnity, but Flint could tell he was excited. Refusing to beg for information, he waited for the revelation. Finally, Ash cleared his throat. "The signal is coming from an origin point approximately one mile below the surface of the ice, a thousand yards inland. In effect, directly below the location of the *Bethany Rose*. Or, rather, its former location."

As Flint remembered what he'd seen in the ship's hold, he felt odd gratitude that it had been smashed to bits.

"You know the local geology better than anyone on my team," Ash said.

"I know the local geology better than anyone on Earth," Flint said.

"I'm glad to hear it. Because we need your help accessing the signal."

"Accessing it? Do you mean drilling?"

"In effect, yes."

Flint felt uneasy. They'd already lost Jurgen.

"You can't bring drill equipment onto that ice. It's suicide. I won't sacrifice any more people."

"I wasn't planning on going in from the top," Ash said.

"Well, you can't dig a hole from Russia."

"What do you know about the geology of the Tenemir trough?"

The Tenemir trough was a feature of the local seabed. The ocean got very deep, very fast. It had been of particular interest to teams of marine biologists studying deep, cold life.

Suddenly, he knew what Ash was planning.

"Surely you can't be thinking of going in from the side."

Ash smiled. "You remember Captain Sanchez?"

Flint sensed there was a third person in the room. She'd been standing near the door so quietly Flint hadn't realized she was there. She had intense eyes under her hair, with a single white streak running from her temple to her ponytail.

"In addition to supervising our fleet of transport craft, she also commands the *Wave Ranger*," Ash explained.

"What's the *Wave Ranger*?" Flint asked. "Have you got a smaller ship in the hold of your ship?"

"And an even smaller ship inside of that one, Doctor Hill. It's ships all the way down," Captain Sanchez said, staring at him so seriously it took him three full seconds to realize she was joking. Grinning, she slid her phone out of her pocket and pulled up a photo.

The *Wave Ranger* was a research vessel. A nice one, by the looks of it. He would have to keep her away from his scientists lest they die of jealousy.

Rear Admiral Ash cleared his throat again, sounding, for the first time since Flint had met him, hesitant. There was a knock at the door, soft but insistent. Ash sighed and went over to open it.

If Flint had known he was about to be the star of an all-staff meeting, he would have put something on that closed in the back.

"I'd also like to introduce Doctor Jake Adams," Ash said.

A short man who looked like he was accustomed to being stepped on flicked a finger up to Flint's bed in greeting.

"Doctor Adams is an accomplished physicist in the Sector of Administration for Understanding Comprehensive Extraterrestrial Relations."

Dr. Milroy laughed so hard a little bit of the cocoa she was holding squirted through her nose and onto Flint's blanket. Based on the expression on Dr. Adams's face, as well as the rear admiral's allergy to anything approaching a sense of humor, Flint didn't think he was joking.

"S.A.U.C.E.R.?" Flint said.

Ash met his eyes and refused to look away.

"It's catchy. You'll get used to it," the rear admiral said.

"It's okay," Dr. Adams said. "It's interesting work. And my brother is a puppeteer, so it would be impossible to shame my family. And ladies really do love a uniform. Even one that comes with a tinfoil hat."

Dr. Adams failed to see Captain Sanchez's eyes narrow at these last statements. Or maybe he didn't care. Flint got the strong sense Jake Adams was a man whose love of his job was so much bigger than other people's skepticism that what other people thought only mattered inasmuch as it affected his funding.

Flint thought someone had better ask the obvious question.

"Is that why we're here? You think there are aliens in the ice?"

This time, no one laughed.

"I'm preparing for all conceivable outcomes," Ash said.

"How many people are in S.A.U.C.E.R.?" Julie asked from the chair next to him.

"At the moment, one," Jake said.

Flint worried. If they needed an alien expert, they'd be seriously understaffed.

Suddenly, he remembered the hold of the *Bethany Rose* and the thing he had found inside. A coughing fit wracked his body, subsiding just as Dr. Milroy was about to hustle everyone out. Taking a deep breath, Flint described what he had seen. Ash looked doubtful. Dr. Milroy looked worried. Dr. Adams looked thrilled.

"Don't get your hopes up," Flint said to the small man, who tried to look serious in response. "I don't think it was an alien. It was too human to be an alien. Two arms and two legs, only...wrong."

He heard Dr. Milroy suck in her breath. "That explains some of what Bill found in the captain's logs. He roped a few grad students into photographing the pages and transcribing everything. There was something about one of the crew becoming a monster. I thought it was a figure of speech."

Dr. Adams's eyes blazed with interest. "I'll need copies of those logs if you don't mind."

Flint nodded. "Tell Bill to give you whatever you need."

Ash stood up. "Now that we have deployed the ocean floor base-camp, it's time to start drilling. The submersible leaves in an hour, so we need whatever help you can give us with the geology ASAP."

"I want to go."

Julie hissed. Ash didn't even meet Flint's gaze.

"That won't be possible."

"Those are my conditions. Whatever else is happening here, I want a front-row seat."

"Why?" Ash asked, sounding suspicious. Flint stammered.

"I haven't lost many people out here," Flint said. "Jurgen was the best of the best, and I want to know why he died."

"If you can convince Doctor Milroy, I'll allow it," Ash finally said.

Julie glared at Flint with so much anger it almost concealed her fear. "If you die in the middle of the ocean, I'll fish your body out and re-feed it to whatever sharks didn't get it the first time."

As it turned out, the *Wave Ranger* wasn't trapped inside the *Taft*, but rather, anchored behind it. The larger vessel's hull had blocked it from the view of the research station. *It's better that way. If the scientists on the station saw this thing, they'd start begging me for one.*

They reached the *Wave Ranger* across a questionable gangplank. Captain Sanchez, back at home on the ship under her command, grew more relaxed as she guided Flint around the edge of the ship. It was smaller than the *Taft*, but it wasn't small. Finally, Sanchez drew up to a halt in front of a small, bulbous submersible, which had a futuristic oblong shape meant to withstand pressures at incredible depths. Flint looked up at the captain.

"So you *do* have a smaller ship inside your ship," Flint said.

"No cat, though," Sanchez said, smiling. "Now, we're running short on time. One of my petty officers is going to give you an abbreviated safety briefing about your submersible trip on the *Devilfish*. The gist of that lecture is if you get sick or injured down there, we won't be able to fly you out for medical attention until you decompress."

"The bends," Flint said.

"I've seen men with the bends before. It's brutal."

"Always men?" Flint asked.

Sanchez shrugged. "Women don't assume they're tougher than a small bubble of nitrogen."

Flint nodded. "If I get sick, hopefully Doctor Milroy will be here since she is the best there is. Will you also be taking the plunge, Captain?"

Sanchez nodded curtly, and two weathered-looking sailors pulled Flint away for his safety briefing.

At the hour on the dot, Flint was inside the little sardine can hold of the *Devilfish*, with Captain Sanchez and two of her men.

"The rear admiral's not joining us?" Flint asked. Sanchez looked at him sternly.

"If the rear admiral leaves, who will steer the *Taft*?"

There was a long pause, then Sanchez and her team burst out laughing. Flint, who had briefly imagined the Admiral at the wheel of some kind of 17th-century frigate, realized Sanchez would be a formidable opponent if he didn't make her an ally.

The vessel shook uncomfortably as the mechanical whine of the crane arm extending them out over the water drowned out their conversation. Flint's arthritis had been manageable for the last few days, maybe rising to the occasion of his new military collaboration, and he sent out a prayer to Poseidon and anyone else who was listening that the pain would stay low and steady for a few more days.

He had seen a few research crews use submersibles, mostly unmanned. The scientists tended to treat these devices like fussy prima donna opera singers, only worth the trouble because, at the end of the day, nothing else could do the job.

The ride got a lot more comfortable once they were underwater, the shaking and jostling giving way to a slow, steady sway.

There was a tiny porthole in the side of the submersible. As Flint watched the ultramarine sea beyond the plexiglass get darker and darker, he wondered what was waiting for them out below the ice.

CHAPTER 15

THE BATHROOM LIGHT FLICKERED briefly then steadied. Referring to the space as a modest-sized bathroom was generous at best, but Eva was grateful nonetheless for the hospitality afforded by her old friend. She closed the door gently behind her, turned the faucet, and let the water run cold before splashing her face, the shock of it grounding her for a few precious seconds.

Her ears were ringing in the silence. The place was almost too quiet.

She looked up at the mirror.

For a moment, she thought she looked worn out but fine. Just pale. Just tired. Last night had been brutal—no sleep, always moving, always watching—but what choice did she have? She leaned in, gripping the porcelain sink tighter as she studied her reflection.

That's when she saw it.

At the edge of her left eye, beneath the skin, a faint iridescence—like oil on water. Not quite a color. Not quite *real*. It shimmered when she tilted her head. She tried to blink it away. It was still there.

Her breath caught. She reached up and ran her fingers across her cheekbone. The skin felt...wrong. Too smooth. Not soft—almost *glassy*.

She looked closer. Pores were gone. The texture was changing. Not all over, just in patches. Like a mask slowly forming beneath the surface.

She exhaled, shaky, and pushed back her damp hair.

That's when the first strand came loose.

It drifted down like a feather, clinging briefly to her hand. Then another. And another.

Eva froze.

She ran her fingers through her scalp again—gently, carefully—and this time, three more hairs came away. Her stomach twisted. Not clumps. Not yet. But enough to know this wasn't stress. This wasn't exhaustion.

The flute?

She looked down at her arms. The veins were more vivid now, branching out across her forearms in delicate, spiraling lines. They pulsed faintly, and she swore—*swore*—they weren't following her blood vessels anymore. They were forming patterns. Geometries.

The same ones carved into the bone.

She leaned over the sink and gripped the edge until her knuckles turned white. The porcelain felt cold, grounding. But the thing in her pack—wrapped in canvas, nestled in a coat at the foot of Gucci's guest bed—it was still *warm*.

It was always warm.

She squeezed her eyes shut, then opened them. The mirror offered no comfort. Only proof.

"I'm changing," she whispered.

Her reflection stared back, silent and still, a stranger with familiar eyes—and something ancient waking behind them.

As usual, Gucci had provided her with an utterly impractical change of clothes—high-waisted cashmere shorts and something on top that appeared to be a cross between a blouse and the inside of a kaleidoscope. Eva poked at a hidden ruffle, trying to feel *au courant* instead of ridiculous.

Gucci remained occupied in his little nest of cables and equipment. He gave her an approving once-over and then looked back at his screen as Eva discreetly confirmed the artifact was still safe in her pack.

"I hope we're not going anywhere. I'm not exactly inconspicuous," Eva said.

"Inconspicuous people are boring," Gucci said.

"I'd rather be boring than dead."

"Boring people are already dead on the inside, *minha linda.*"

"Did you find anything out about Wulf?" Eva asked.

"I read through all his emails from the week before he died. Fantastically melo-dramatic. Did you know he was sleeping with three of his graduate students?"

Eva rolled her eyes. "Did you find anything out about Wulf that would *surprise* anyone?"

"Unfortunately, no."

"Hm. He was being careful, I guess. You know, he sent me a package."

"How retro."

Because Gucci had no windows, Eva had to content herself with staring into one of his abstract paintings.

"I need to leave the country."

Gucci nodded. "I take it you're planning on asking for a bigger favor than an uber to the airport."

"I have a gut feeling that if I pop back up in regular society, I'll be dead in days," Eva said.

"Always trust your gut," Gucci responded approvingly. "I have a solution, but it won't be cheap or nice."

"I'd never come to you for cheap and nice," Eva said.

"Someone I have sex with sometimes has a four-seater plane. If I ask nicely, he might be willing to accept a fat wad of cash to take you out of the country."

Eva felt her stomach drop as she considered the state of her bank account. She'd be able to keep her head above water if the check from the Amazon cleared.

"Call your friend," she said. There was no avoiding it.

"We're not friends. He works in finance. Can you imagine?"

An image of a considerable corner office with a vast stretch of mahogany desk overtook Eva's vision.

"Sounds dreadful," she said.

CHAPTER 16

THE GENTLE SWAY OF the submersible and aquamarine light trickling through the porthole lulled Flint into a lucid sleep, and he was jolted awake by the sound of his own snoring.

Captain Sanchez and her men were laughing.

"Don't worry. It's common," Sanchez said. "Something about the pressure and the light. I've always said insomniacs should buy themselves submersibles. Anyway, you're just in time for the big show."

She pointed out the porthole. The glass was cool on Flint's face as he pressed against it.

There was some kind of dome on the sea floor, glowing with lights. Some kind of marine specimen collection device?

As they approached, he realized the dome was much bigger than that.

The Devilfish's pilot cut through the silence. "We are approaching the Hab. Contact in two hundred meters. One hundred eighty—"

"Hab?" Flint said. "Is that what you call it?"

"Short for habitat," Captain Sanchez said.

"When was it built? I'm surprised our marine biology teams haven't noticed it."

"It's a mobile, modular station," Sanchez said. "It only takes a couple days to place. When we're done using it here, we simply let out the ballast and scoop it up when it floats to the surface. We have to send the people up on a sub to decompress, of course."

Flint, who had watched a few decades of science teams beg, borrow, and occasionally steal equipment for their modestly funded projects, felt a wash of annoyance at the military's boundless resources.

"Seventy. Sixty. Fifty," the pilot said.

"I appreciate you showing me your fancy toys," Flint said. The sound of metal on metal echoed through the *Devilfish*.

"We are docked with the habitat," the pilot said. "The airlock will be empty in a few minutes."

"Thank you," Sanchez said, staring at the exit port like she was encouraging it to drain faster. She looked back at Flint.

"Welcome to the Hab."

THE HUGE MASS OF water surrounding the Hab seemed to press in on Flint, a constant clamminess that made his skin itch. He only liked water when it was ice, snow, or coffee; the few times he'd had to go to and from the mainland by boat, he'd talked Dr. Milroy into prescribing him a racehorse's dosage of tranquilizers. He wondered if this place was meant to be a watery jail where he could be monitored and weakened until his research station could be brushed off the ice with a flick of the wrist. It quickly became apparent, however, he had something to contribute.

Rear Admiral Ash's voice crackled over the comms in the control room, a chilly den of screens and wires.

"If you break my drill bit, I'll have you court-martialed," he said.

Flint stared at the geologic data on the screen in front of him.

"Are you sure about this?" the young lieutenant sitting next to him asked. The man's name was Smith or Schmidt or something equally unmemorable. "Although I'm pretty sure he can't court-martial a civilian."

"I'm sure," Flint said.

The lieutenant pulled a small case of bright orange earplugs out of his pocket and offered them to Flint, who accepted them gratefully. He felt even more grateful a second later when a colossal rumble of metal on stone shook the station as the drill bit on the rig outside began chewing through bedrock.

"You're sure that binary signal isn't coming from that old sailing ship?" Flint shouted. The young lieutenant watched his lips carefully.

"Definitely not! I'd bet money whatever's behind the signal is responsible for wrecking her, though."

"You think it's that old?" Flint shouted.

The lieutenant shrugged, clearly trying to avoid any more chit-chat. Flint smiled, nodded, and left the kid to his work.

CHAPTER 17

Eva woke up in the middle of the night in a blind panic. Her bed was so perfect, and her sheets were so soft it took something monumental to catapult her out of dreamland. That something was the realization that the jeans she had given to one of Gucci's impeccably trained maids had held the thumb drive from Wulf. Imagining it going round and round in a washing machine, she sat bolt upright and ran for the door of her room.

There was a metallic noise as she ran. A jangling she couldn't put her finger on until cold metal bit into her ankle, and she fell flat on her face. She screamed as her nose slammed onto the stained concrete floor with an unpleasant crunch.

When the pain died down enough for her to think straight, Eva sat up and prodded her ankle. There was a sinking feeling in the pit of her stomach as she realized someone had put a sturdy metal cuff around her left ankle. The shackle was connected to a long silver chain padlocked to a bolt just out of sight under her bed. Eva noted someone had wrapped a Hermes scarf around her ankle so the metal wouldn't rub against her bare skin.

Gucci's home wasn't a mansion with traditional rooms, so Eva wasn't in a traditional bedroom. Instead of rooms, Gucci had constructed small islands throughout his huge open space that gestured at parlors, kitchens, and bedrooms. Last night, he had put Eva to bed in one of these islands, a palatial circular bed ringed by tall bookshelves. Eva, who had only sometimes worked with books during her antiquities career, had found most people who wanted to own pretty, valuable old books didn't much care what those books were. Gucci was different.

The books on these shelves were both color-coordinated and carefully curated, which must have taken incredible effort. Probably, he had just hired someone.

Footsteps echoed on the concrete beyond the bookshelves, and a moment later, Gucci, looking monkish in saffron silk pajamas, loomed over her.

"I heard someone running! Why were you running?" Gucci said, looking as alarmed as Eva felt about the blood pouring out of her nose onto his expensive floor.

"I left a thumb drive in my jeans. I remembered it in the middle of the night. I hope you didn't wash it."

Gucci looked guilty, staring at the shackle on her ankle.

"I didn't wash it. I decoded it."

"Is that why I'm chained to your bed?"

"Don't be tawdry. You're chained to *a* bed. And yes. The contents of the thumb drive led me to take that unfortunate precaution. I'm sorry about your nose. I didn't anticipate midnight sprinting on your part."

"How did you get this thing on me without waking me up?" Eva asked, poking at the shackle.

"Infinite thread count sheets and microclimate temperature control. Also, the bags under your eyes yesterday had practically turned into luggage trunks, so I put a mild sedative in your creme anglaise last night."

Eva scowled. This is what she got for eating dairy. Was that why she was feeling so woozy? "What was on the thumb drive? Are you selling me to the people who tried to kill me or something?"

"I suppose I could. But it wouldn't be...stylish. I have a hacker's natural hunger for information. I opened that thumb drive–which was NOT easy, believe me. Now I have a can full of worms I don't understand."

"You chained me to a bed so I would explain worms to you?" Eva said.

The edges of the pool of blood on the concrete floor beneath her were starting to go fuzzy. Gucci's bed was comfortable, but it wasn't nearly as comfortable as this cold concrete. Eva smiled as the floor floated helpfully up to meet her face, cradling her head. She didn't remember lying down, but she was staring up at a forest of bookshelves. Her eyes caught the title on the spine of a cobalt leather book on a bottom shelf. *A Midsummer Night's Dream*. How appropriate. As she stared at the book, her consciousness thinned into nothingness.

CHAPTER 18

WHEN THE DRILL BIT broke, the sound was less jarring than the silence that followed. After hours of the constant roar, the air around Flint felt strangely empty.

Popping out of his bunk, he saw Captain Sanchez walking rapidly toward him.

"They want you in the drill bay!" she said, too loud, before apologizing and adjusting her volume.

"Ash threatened to court martial us if we broke his drill bit," he said nervously.

Sanchez's eyebrows rose. She grinned and shrugged. "Don't worry. The brig's plenty comfortable."

Flint found himself wanting to hear the story of how she knew what the brig was like. Perhaps over hot toddies under a down blanket. Instead, he nodded curtly and headed down the hallway.

Inside the control room, a terrified tech handed him a phone. "Rear Admiral Ash for you, sir. Er, I mean, Doctor."

Flint smiled at the woman and took the receiver.

"Explain what's happening," Ash barked over the line.

"Well, I just got down here, Vernon, but either the world's largest pair of fingernails scraped across a chalkboard or our drill bit broke."

He took a moment to glance at the screens in front of him, staring at them until the information they contained started to assemble itself in his brain. "You'll be happy to learn—I think—we broke the drill *on* something. Also, you can't court-martial me. I googled it."

There was a long pause, where the rear admiral appeared to be selecting an extremely specific invective. Finally, he spoke. "What did we break the bit on?"

Flint looked back at the data screens. Good question.

"There was a sudden change in gradation from bedrock to, er—"

"What?"

"Don't laugh at me, Admiral."

"I never laugh."

Flint believed it. "I think it might be diamond."

"We broke a two-million-dollar drill bit on a diamond? We better be talking about a celebrity-engagement-sized rock."

Flint let out a deep breath as he watched a few of the drill techs exchange a look.

"It's slightly bigger than that, Rear Admiral. I think it's a layer.

"A layer over what?"

"I thought it was flat at first. But that's because we're not seeing much of it. There's actually a slight curvature to it."

Flint paused for long enough that Ash asked if he was still there.

"Yeah, yeah. I'm here. This might seem a little hard to believe, but if the curvature is the same everywhere, we're looking at a massive dome. About a mile and a half in diameter."

"You broke my drill bit on a mile-high spherical diamond?"

Rear Admiral Ash was clearly struggling with this information.

"I doubt the whole thing is made of that material. But I don't know. It's extremely dense. The radar won't penetrate it."

There was a pause before Ash spoke. "Put someone in my chain of command on the phone."

Flint handed the receiver to the least terrified-looking person in arms' reach, a petty officer named Carver.

"Sir!" Carver said, snapping to attention. "We are considering all possibilities, sir, but Doctor Hill's proposition fits the existing data better than any alternative theory presently known, sir!"

Flint wondered if Ash could tell whether his people were standing at attention over the phone. Probably. Carver placed the phone back on its receiver.

"We're sending a dive team down the shaft," he said.

Flint hoped there was a good reason to send human beings into a long cold hole at the bottom of the world.

Gucci's round, worried face hovered in Eva's vision.

"The nose isn't broken, *meu bem*. Although if you want to say it is as an excuse to get a little work done, you'll never hear a peep from me."

Eva touched her nose gently with one finger, then quickly retracted it after a starburst of pain nearly knocked her back into unconsciousness.

When her eyes were fully open again, Gucci handed her a bone china teacup of espresso.

"Aren't you supposed to be giving me water or chicken soup or something?"

"Caffeinate up, and I'll let you see what was on that thumb drive."

"And what happens after that?" Eva asked.

"We'll...see."

She drank the coffee. Then asked for another as she scrolled through a secured laptop Gucci brought her full of data from the thumb drive. He perched at the edge of her bed.

"It's some kind of code, but nothing I've seen before. Huge blocks of repeating letters."

"If it's a code, then you're in a better position to solve it than me," Eva said, resisting the urge to scratch her nose. "I'm no expert cryptographer."

"That's true. But you know more about Wulf's secret little project. And I suspect this may be related to your work in the Amazon and research at Sao Paulo University."

Eva, who hadn't given Gucci that much information, narrowed her eyes. He broke her gaze and looked down at his Balenciaga sneakers.

"You're right. I snooped, sue me. But there's still one thing I don't under-stand."

Eva cocked an eyebrow. Gucci watched her face closely. "How is this all con-nected to Antarctica?" he asked.

Antarctica? She'd never done anything in Antarctica. There weren't many antiquities down there because there weren't many people. She'd never even en-countered anyone offering to sell pieces of Amundsen's snowsuit, Robert Scott's beard clippings, or vials of melted South Pole snow.

Eva looked down at the screen of the tablet. There was a huge mass of letters dotted with periodic time stamps.

"What's in Antarctica?" she asked, genuinely curious.

"I don't know," Gucci said, looking suddenly huffy. "You're supposed to tell me that. I sent out a few petabytes of spiders to crawl the global data networks to try to find a match to the information on this thumb drive. I got exactly one ping. One. Do you know how rare it is? No one on this planet has secrets anymore. At least not from me. Well, no one except for a single computer somewhere on the frozen wasteland. No one's writing a paper about it or sending any emails. The information is just sitting there. I want to know what it means."

Two hours later, Eva called Gucci back to her bedside.

"In a sense, you're right about this being a code. It's a DNA sequence. A very fine-grained DNA sequence. We're talking about the entire human genome."

"That's a lot of data."

"Yes. It is. In fact, it's more than a lot of data. Because we're not looking at just one sequence. It's a time series. A single organism's DNA changes over time."

"I thought DNA only changes on the macro level? Over millions of years. The double helix can't just have a midlife crisis and decide to change careers."

"That's true. Normally, anyways. The type of mutation this data shows could *possibly* be caused by extreme radiation sickness. But given the level of teratogenic damage, I'm surprised this person survived long enough for their DNA to change so extensively. They're almost certainly dead now."

"You're sure it's a human? Not, what, a baboon? Don't we share something like 90% of our DNA?"

"98.8%. But no, this has all the markers of a human. Or...they *were* human when this process started."

"So, what are they now?"

It was a good question. Eva thought about Dr. Martin, coughing up blood. She thought about the bone flute, its effect on those who have had contact with it. And what about her own exposure to the Amazonian artifact?

Were the same processes that had disfigured the person in this data going on inside of her? Was she, too, being remade at the cellular level? She didn't feel sick, aside from the smashed nose. She didn't feel different at all.

Eva shut the laptop and stared at the ceiling.

"Can you isolate the changing sequences from the static ones? I have a hunch."

"I'll see what I can do. Now, what do you want for lunch? I'll order in."

CHAPTER 19

THE DIVERS HADN'T BEEN able to confirm Flint's diamond hypothesis. In fact, the divers hadn't been able to confirm anything because the object that had broken the drill bit had resisted every sampling attempt the divers made.

"Aren't you one of America's preeminent geologists? How come you can't tell me anything?" There was an edge in the rear admiral's voice, although Flint suspected it had more to do with the situation than it did with his work.

"Science only has answers for the questions scientists have asked," Flint said. "At this point, we're pretty deep in unasked questions. Diamond is still my best guess."

"It sure as hell doesn't look like a diamond."

That was true. The footage captured by the divers had shown a smooth, matte gray surface at the end of the drill shaft. The surface showed no seams, pockmarks, or even color gradations.

"I'm tempted to requisition the most expensive laser the Navy owns and cut a hole in whatever it is."

"You could certainly try," Flint said. "Although it's worth considering whether the unusual material was designed as some kind of containment device."

"For what?" Ash said.

"Something that needed containing." Flint was enjoying playing cool to Ash's hot, but truthfully, he felt uneasy. "Have you ever heard about the WIPP?" Flint asked.

"No."

"It's the Waste Isolation Pilot Project. Basically, it was the Department of Energy's attempt to create a marker for a radioactive waste dump. They wanted it to last for thousands of years, even if human civilization collapsed and no one could speak English anymore."

"So what did they do? Put up a bunch of drawings of a little stick-figure man dying of radiation poisoning?"

"Yes. But that wasn't their only idea. They had one plan that was never aired in public. The team thought the best answer might be to put a small amount of radioactive waste in a shielded box on the surface. A little taste, if you will, of what lay below."

"Wouldn't that be dangerous if someone who didn't understand what was in the box opened it?"

"Exactly. If someone three thousand years in the future opened the box, they would die of radiation poisoning. But that was the point. It's hard to ignore a warning that comes with dead bodies."

"So, you think that's what the vessel might be? A box full of death warning us not to dig deeper?"

"I have no idea what it is. Opening it up would probably give us more information. But that information might come at a cost we're not prepared to pay."

"What do you propose?"

The smooth, black surface, buried under rock and water, tugged magnetically at Flint's curiosity.

"I say we keep digging. We've only looked at a sliver of the exterior. So we excavate. We keep trying to get a sample. Eventually, even if we can't get a sample, we'll have a hole big enough to bring equipment into. Either way, we get our analysis."

On the comm screen, Ash's face was so still Flint briefly thought the connection had dropped. After a second, however, Ash nodded curtly.

"Do it." The comm line cut.

Everyone stared at Flint.

"You heard the rear admiral. Replace the bit and drill, baby, drill."

Gucci continued to be cheerful and attentive, but he brushed off her requests to unlock the chain around her ankle as if she had asked him to wear an ironic t-shirt to a black-tie wedding. Two nights after she'd first found herself chained up, she took a comprehensive inventory of her surroundings.

Unfortunately, the place was spotless. No hapless butler had left bolt cutters beneath the bed or metal-etching acid in the nightstand. The laptops Gucci brought her weren't networked. If Gucci had a phone, he didn't bring it near her bed.

She knew he wasn't getting a perverse thrill out of holding her captive, and she didn't think he was holding her for ransom, either. Maybe it was simpler than that. He had a mystery, and she had answers. *He would probably slit my throat if he thought he would find something interesting inside it.*

The only thing left was the books. Because she had to start somewhere, Eva started with the cobalt blue *A Midsummer Night's Dream*, thumbing through the pages, putting it back, and picking up the book next to it.

Two bookshelves and several paper cuts later, she found her salvation. A tiny travel-sized tool kit flattened between the pages of a first-edition copy of *A Christmas Carol*. Someone must have stuck it in there as a makeshift bookmark and then forgotten about it. The kit contained a small but sturdy pin Eva tested for strength against the bedpost before slipping it into the keyhole of her ankle cuff.

Hearing footsteps, she stuck the pin into the nearest corner of her mattress and opened *A Christmas Carol* to a random location.

"Interesting choice for August," Gucci said, staring at the cover of the book. "Taking a little break when you should be working on my data?"

"I'd be more effective if you unchained me and paid me a salary."

Gucci rolled his eyes.

"I'm sending one of the shop girls on a coffee run. Want anything?"

"Just regular coffee," Eva said.

The second he was gone, she went back to wiggling the needle in her ankle cuff. The inner workings of the shackle jangled, and she prayed the needle would hold. Three minutes later, she heard a *click*.

CHAPTER 20

FOR EIGHT DAYS, THE drill team's excavation work slowly uncovered identical swaths of smooth, gray, diamond-hard material.

On the ninth day, the team found a door.

More accurately, they found a thin circular seam in the gray material, which circumscribed an area approximately four feet in diameter.

Thinking about the relationship of an average human door to an average human, Flint wondered what kind of organism would use a door with such a shape.

The door didn't have a handle or a keyhole. Instead, in the center of the circle, there was a six-inch diameter rough patch. When examined under a portable aquatic microscope, the rough patch turned out to be a panel covered in millions of silicon threads. According to the chemistry team, each individual thread was one nanometer wide and nine nanometers in length. They were packed together at even intervals, like hair.

"When you say 'hair,' you're not talking about an organism, are you?" Ash asked. He still hadn't come down to the Hab.

"No, I think it was manufactured, not grown. But hair comes close. The door basically has a nanoscale buzz cut."

"For what?" Ash asked. Good question.

"I think it's a lock," Captain Sanchez said from over Flint's shoulder.

He turned around to see her staring intently at his screen.

"I was about to tell him," Flint said with a surly undertone.

"What makes you think it's a lock?" Ash asked.

"Doors don't have many functions beyond selective admissions. Assuming it *is* a door," Sanchez said.

"It's as good a guess as any," Flint added.

"Not a guess, sir. More, a deduction based on the best information we have," Sanchez shot him an irritated look.

"Okay," Ash said. "Let's assume it's a lock."

"Yes, sir."

"So...where's the key?"

CHAPTER 21

EVA LEFT THE SHACKLES on but unlatched until the next time Gucci asked her what she wanted for lunch. Then, padding silently in bare feet across the polished concrete, she made her way through the labyrinth of bookshelves surrounding her bed and peered into Gucci's vast domain. Spotting the back of his head on his sofa, encased by studded noise-canceling headphones, she went back to her bed, set her tablet to play some music, slipped *A Christmas Carol* and a few other expensive volumes into the oversized pockets of her silk pajamas, grabbed her backpack and moved as quickly as she could toward the tunnel that ran to his boutique. The darkness closed in around her, bare feet felt exposed as she wiggled her way through, only to find a grate covering the far end. She backed up through the tunnel and found a hiding spot behind a polished onyx plinth onto which a concealed A/V system projected an eclectic mix of dubstep music videos and nature documentary footage. Eva scanned the ceiling.

At least he's too paranoid to allow security cameras in here.

Gucci stayed on his tech island, fully absorbed in his digital world. Eva, sitting on cold concrete against even colder stone, had just started to shiver when she heard a noise in the tunnel. A scrape, then the fibrous tear of fabric and a young woman's voice swearing softly in Portuguese.

Eva untied the scarf around her ankle and tensed for action.

Emerging from the tunnel, Gucci's assistant flung a large paper bag of food on the ground with evident distaste and turned her full attention to the three-inch tear in her sequined jumpsuit. It was not an outfit optimized for tunnel rats.

Feeling a sharp stab of adrenaline rise from her stomach to her throat, Eva struck.

She knocked the woman to the floor with a knee to the small of her back. The woman let out a single shriek as Eva wrapped the silk scarf around her neck, cutting off her air supply.

The woman clawed at her neck, but Eva was stronger. As her muscles burned with the strain, she caught a glimpse of Gucci's unmoving head out of the corner of her eye. *The best noise-canceling headphones money can buy.* A brief current of jealousy ran through her. She wished *she* was so rich she couldn't hear her captives escaping.

The struggling body beneath her collapsed into a motionless but still breathing lump. Eva barely had time to think before an urgent drive took over, and she found herself scrambling through the tunnel to freedom. A sinking feeling clawed at her as she saw the darkness at the end, but a sigh of relief escaped when she realized it wasn't locked—the door of the armoire had simply been closed. As she kicked the door open with her bare foot, she found herself face to face with one of Gucci's large security guards.

"*Eu ouvi um grito...*" the guard said, staring at the tunnel past Eva's shoulder, then at her.

He must have heard that shout. Eva asked herself what Gucci would do, and drew herself up to her full height.

"Stupid girl tore up her jumpsuit. It's Marchesa. She'll have to resew the sequins by hand. Idiot. Anyway, Gucci said my shoes were an affront to common decency. He threw them away and sent me to get new ones."

HEART POUNDING IN HER chest, Eva strode languidly across the room and slid her feet into a pair of multicolored high-top leather sneakers, rolling her eyes theatrically at the guard as she did up the laces.

The girl at the counter didn't look surprised. The first time Eva had met him, Gucci had gone behind her back and thrown out half her closet. She doubted he'd dropped the habit.

When she'd laced up the shoes, Eva stood up and sighed.

"What's-her-name forgot the coffee, so I'm going for some," she announced and strode casually through the door, smiling at the guard and the girl at the counter. She kept the quiver out of her voice and prayed they couldn't hear her heart hammering in her chest.

She forced herself to make it around the corner of the building before she started sprinting.

The fashion district was surrounded by a less-fashionable district, which turned out to be the perfect place to trade the designer clothes on her body for a serviceable sweatsuit and a short stack of cash. It took her the greater part of a day to hitchhike to the coast and then out to the industrial docks. People kept offering to take her to the beach.

The beach would have been nicer than the clutch of seedy dockside bars she quickly dunked herself in, but she had a surprisingly good time. The (mostly) men she met having their shore leave were multicultural, leaned free-spirited, and were less handsy than she'd feared. It took her thirty-six hours of hard drinking to find a cargo ship captain who *could* help her, a tall, soft-spoken Nigerian who had picked up a fondness for Dickens at Eton. She had to beat him at chess twice to convince him he *should* help her.

Eva wondered if she would have to hide from customs in a plastic tub or bag of laundry, but Captain Musa laughed and told her she just had to stay in her room. "The inspector is a friend of mine. He doesn't go out of his way to look for trouble, and I don't go out of my way to bring it. Usually. I'll make some calls to an old girlfriend whose family runs tours out of Ushuaia. It is not likely she can help you. But it is, at least, *possible*."

Eva raised her eyebrows. "I didn't realize I was just an excuse to call up your ex," she said.

Captain Musa winked at her, tucked the first edition of *A Christmas Carol* into his breast pocket, and patted it possessively, winking at her as he shut her cabin door behind her.

Three hours later, they set sail for Argentina.

CHAPTER 22

FLINT FELT RESTLESS AND annoyed, like when he couldn't finish a Sudoku. He spent a few hours reading through the captain's logs from the *Bethany Rose*, which unsettled him further.

August 2, 1766. I feel now that the cold is stalking us, tensed and coiled, waiting everywhere, but especially beyond the walls of the ship. Perhaps I have gone mad. Perhaps some rescue vessel—or, more likely, opportunistic scavenger—will come to find our bodies, pry open the hold, and find a normal man, untransformed, sane, and whole on a Bedlam boat. By the grace of God, the monster has stopped shouting.

August 4, 1766. We have lost another crew member. Tipton spent the morning screaming that his fingers were longer than usual, and instead of reassuring him, the good Doctor locked himself in his room with half our remaining rations. Tipton vaulted over the railing onto the ice. We heard him longer than we saw him, shouting about transfiguration and alchemy. I think we will never find his body.

The only entries after that were nearly illegible, with the exception of three words underlined on the final page:

GOD SAVE US.

CHAPTER 23

Stymied by the locked door, Flint and Captain Sanchez spent the next few days playing gin rummy in the mess hall. He was so bored he was contemplating asking Ash if he could download *Bonny Seas* and play it over the Navy's comms network when he got a call from Dr. Milroy, checking to see if he'd fully recovered. He was about to tell her his hands were actually doing much better underwater when he saw her frown, staring off above his shoulder.

"Why are you looking at an ear?" she said.

Flint turned around. Behind, on a large projection screen in his office, was a magnified image of the nano-hairs on the door.

"What do you mean?" he said.

"Those are stereo-cilia? Right? Is that a whale or something? It's awfully big for a person."

"What are...what did you say?"

"Stereo-cilia?"

"Right. What is that?"

"They're tiny hairs in the human ear. When a sound wave passes over them, it registers as mechanical motion. Their movement gets translated to the brain as hearing, basically."

Flint suddenly felt idiotic that he hadn't consulted Dr. Milroy about the door. They'd asked every mechanical engineer in a hundred-mile radius.

"I don't think the thing we're trying to get inside is organic. In other words, I don't think it's a big ear."

If it is, I hope it's not listening.

"It could still be mechanical. Have you considered that it's designed to respond to sound waves?"

He hadn't considered it, but he would certainly start. Hanging up the call, he went to find Captain Sanchez.

Eva, who had packed for the equator, was ill-prepared for the freezing temperatures of Ushuaia. Luckily, Eva's host Reya was so grateful to have Captain Musa back in her life that she was struck by a burst of generosity and parted with an old coat and a few pairs of gloves. Even so, Eva spent the next few days in bed, huddled under a duvet, wondering what the hell she was doing. Reya had installed Eva in her apartment with a cupboard full of canned soup, told her not to go anywhere, and gone off with Captain Musa on his trip over to the Falkland Islands. The spark between them was so evident Eva wondered if she had parted with *A Christmas Carol* for nothing.

Three days after Reya had left, promising to help Eva find a berth on a cruise ship to Antarctica when she returned, Eva grew bored of attempting to read Reya's small collection of Spanish poetry and went down to the docks. The houses there were painted bright colors, a cheerful juxtaposition with the landscape's end-of-the-world austerity. She spent some of her dwindling stack of bills on an overpriced glass of wine at what passed for a tourist bar and chatted with the bartender until he ran out of his rudimentary English vocabulary and she ran out of her Spanish.

She was growing concerned about the cumulative effects of exposure to the artifact. Although progressing slowly, her hair loss was evident and not her only symptom. Weakness was setting in, all the walking was leaving her feeling worn out.

Giving up and climbing the hill back to Reya's apartment, Eva realized she was being followed. Not subtly, either. The man was about a foot taller than most of the locals, with black fatigues and a businesslike buzz cut. She tried ducking between a few houses, but the town was too small for someone unfamiliar with the territory to lose a tail.

Cursing, she looped her way back to the docks and settled for standing in the middle of the busiest road she could find. Her shadow lingered in a nearby doorway, looking at his phone.

"Hey!" she shouted.

Mr. Buzzcut looked up, not seeming terribly surprised.

"I want to talk to you."

A few fishermen watched her with open curiosity. The man made his way to the middle of the street.

"Who sent you? What do you want?" she demanded.

"My friend told me an American woman with no passport was looking for a ride to Antarctica." He was American, with no trace of a regional accent.

Eva relaxed a little. Maybe Reya had sent him to scoop her up for the final leg of the trip.

"Can you get me there?" she asked.

The man's answering smile was neither threatening nor reassuring.

"In a sense, I can," he said, fishing a wallet out of his pocket. When he opened it, it took the badge a moment to register in her brain. "Petty Officer Ronald Syl, Ma'am. U.S. Naval Intelligence. I'd like you to come with me."

ON THE ONE HAND, Eva hadn't been assassinated. And she had only barely been abducted, escorted courteously on and off a series of increasingly larger boats. On the other hand, the naval intelligence officers she had dealt with had confiscated everything but her underwear, given her no information, and questioned her intensely about her activities since she'd arrived in Brazil.

Eventually, she found herself in a tiny but reasonably comfortable crew cabin. The door wasn't locked, but it was guarded by some extremely athletic-looking young sailors who politely told her she was not welcome to move about the ship.

They did, however, provide her with above-average coffee and after the first day, a couple of paperback mysteries.

The officers who had interrogated her hadn't exactly accused her of lying, but they did keep finding new ways to ask the same questions until she was too exhausted to tell them anything but the unvarnished truth. They seemed appropriately alarmed when she told them about the bone flute's origins up in the jungle, although her questions about where they were keeping it were answered with silence, which told her she was not getting the flute back any time soon.

The only thing she didn't tell them about was Wulf's thumb drive and the data set on it. She didn't have it, and she didn't know what it meant. Besides, it never hurt to keep a bargaining chip in your bra.

On her fourth day of genteel captivity, Eva was picking at a plate of surprisingly good shrimp and grits when there was a knock at her door.

The knock was a courtesy—the door would open whether she answered it or not—but Eva did answer it and found herself staring slightly down at a serious-looking man in black fatigues.

"Good afternoon, Doctor Ward. I hope your stay aboard my ship hasn't been too uncomfortable."

Eva made a noncommittal noise. Surely if they had decided to fling her overboard, they would have sent someone less important. Eva looked down and reluctantly shook the offered hand.

"Your coffee is better than I expected," she said finally. This got a small smile.

"My name is Rear Admiral Vernon Ash, and I am here on behalf of the United States Government to request your assistance in an urgent matter."

"You're sending down a *prisoner*?" Flint asked, incredulous. When had Ash found the time to take prisoners?

"There's no place more secure than the Hab. Captain Sanchez hasn't had a breakout yet. Besides, at this point, I'm choosing to think of her more as an archaeology attaché."

"I'm not sure you can trust someone to cooperate when you've been interrogating them in a grimy little cell for a week."

"She was in vacant officers' quarters, not the brig," Ash said. "Anyway, she's from your world. University brainiac. See what you make of her."

"She's not a geologist," Flint said. "From what you've told me, it sounds like she's barely even been in the field."

"You'll figure it out. Do whatever intellectuals do. Complain about your grad students. I don't know. Let me know if she says anything interesting."

"You mean spy on her," Flint said.

"I mean, put your heads together and try to solve the problem."

"Try to open the door."

"The door. The ear. Whatever it is."

Ash hung up the call, and Flint caught sight of his own reflection in the black screen. He had a sudden urge to comb his hair. He still wasn't entirely sure if he was supposed to be a host or a babysitter.

FOR THE FIRST TIME in days, Eva felt like she wasn't teetering on the edge of a dangerous precipice. Remarkably, she was feeling somewhat back to her normal self. Her arms and skin no longer looked so strange. *That was some power nap.*

She hadn't been keelhauled or arrested for obscure violations of maritime law, and now she was being sent under the ocean to "assess an object of national importance." Most of her meager possessions had been laundered and returned to her, and the quartermaster had provided her with a full set of Navy-issued snow gear. They hadn't given her back the bone flute, although, in a rare moment of information-sharing, Ash told her he was sending it down with her to the Hab.

In other words, things had settled down, and despite her best efforts to stay alert for the novelty of her first submersible trip, she slept the whole way down. When the exceedingly competent and surprisingly likable Captain Sanchez tapped her on the shoulder, the airlock was already open.

Eva blinked and yawned, the narrow scramble into the Hab reminding her of the entrance to Gucci's lair. Looking at the damp walls, she doubted much couture awaited her at the end of this one.

A small knot of people assembled in the docking bay. Three were cut from the same military cloth, buttoned up with polished shoes. The fourth man was different, silver haired with bad posture and his hands stuffed into his pockets. She felt a small current of annoyance as she realized he reminded her of Sigmund Wulf. She almost took a step backward, but the space was tiny, and there was nowhere to go.

The group approached her.

"Welcome to the Hab, Doctor Ward. I'm Petty Officer Jered." One of the young military men shook her hand succinctly and introduced the other crew. Finally, the silver-haired man stepped forward.

"Doctor Flint Hill," he said, declining to put his hand out. Eva wondered if he was a germaphobe or simply an asshole. "You wanna settle in, or you wanna see why Ash dunked you in the bottom of the Weddell Ocean?"

Eva felt herself warming to this scruffy, fatherly man. Maybe he wasn't like Wulf after all. The first time Wulf had met her, he hadn't shaken her hand, either. Instead, he'd slipped it under her blouse onto her lower back.

"I had a nap on the *Devilfish*, so we may as well get to it," she said, smiling. "Lead the way, Doctor Hill."

CHAPTER 24

Flint knew Ash wouldn't have sent Dr. Ward down unless her credentials were impeccable. Still, she seemed out of place, like a plucked macaw, her clothes drab and joyless. She looked, frankly, a bit snobbish for cramped military quarters. Well. Perhaps she could steal some of these decorated officers' medals and turn them into festive earrings. And he recognized the look on her face. He was used to seeing it on researchers and their techs right before they started making mistakes. Sheer, unadulterated exhaustion.

Flint decided to stop worrying. Dr. Ward couldn't screw up simply *looking* at the door. He would try to get her alone to make sure the Navy hadn't roughed her up or woken her up every two hours until she talked or anything like that. He didn't think so, but you could never be too sure.

In the control room, amidst the screens and instrument panels, Flint watched as Dr. Ward looked around. Confusion flickered across her face as she scanned the desks and floor. She was looking for something.

"Well, where is it?" she said finally. Flint coughed.

"Oh. I thought...I'm sorry, Doctor Ward, I didn't realize. I assumed Ash had told you something. The artifact isn't here. It's out there."

He struggled to choose a direction to point in and, after a bit of hand waving, landed on a spot somewhere over Dr. Ward's shoulder. She glanced behind her at where he was pointing, which turned out to be a sticky note that read, "TELL ASH TO STOP BUYING THE SHITTY PENCILS."

"I prefer a nice fountain pen," she said mildly.

"Well, you're out of luck. Pens explode in the pressure down here. Sorry. Let me show you a picture."

He sat down at the station he had started to think of as *his* and pulled up an image of the alien door.

"Calling it an *artifact* is a bit of an understatement. What we're looking at is really a structure. A big one. About a mile and a half in diameter buried under thousands of feet of ice. The dome—so far, everything we've uncovered has had identical curvature—is made of a rigid material we have not been able to identify."

"Have you found any entrances? Gates? Garbage chutes? Ceremonial vents?" Her face looked contemplative as she stared at the screen.

"We think we found a door."

He pulled up a magnified image, pointing out the threads and explaining what Dr. Milroy had told him. "We think it can be unlocked with some kind of sound."

He felt crazy as he said it. He probably could have eased into it a bit better. Concision might not be a strength when there was this much to take in.

Eva inhaled a few deep breaths as she stared at the image of the door. She whispered under her breath.

"The flute."

"What?" Flint said.

Eva smiled. "Doctor Hill. It's time to pay the piper."

EVA DIDN'T HAVE AN ear for music. Once every few years, she developed a burning need to play a song in her car at maximum volume fifty times in a row. But outside of that, she mostly listened to the news.

And yet, when she told Flint Hill the artifact she'd encountered in the Amazon, the one associated with weird data that matched the signal coming from this site, might be a flute, he looked at her like he expected her to play it.

"I've never played anything more impressive than 'Hot Cross Buns,' and even that was a while ago," she said. Flint turned to Captain Sanchez, who had been brought in on the conversation primarily because she was the only one in the Hab who knew the code to the lockbox where Eva's bone flute was stored.

"Are there any musicians down here?" he asked.

The captain stared contemplatively at Eva.

"I think Ensign Rawlings was in a ska band," she said.

"He said *musicians*," Eva said, watching the corner of the captain's lip quirk up. "Preferably one with woodwinds experience."

The captain nodded curtly, turned, and left.

A few minutes later, a voice crackled over the loudspeaker.

"Captain Sanchez for all the crew. I have an unusual request, but this is not a drill, and it is not a joke. If anyone has any experience with woodwind instrume nts...flutes, oboes, recorders, pan pipes, anything, you are ordered to report to the control room immediately. Once again, anyone with any amount of woodwinds experience. Thank you. Sanchez out."

Sanchez returned, and almost immediately, two sailors presented themselves at the control room. One looked sick as he explained to Sanchez he had played the flute from third to sixth grade, worrying at one of the buttons on his sleeve. He apologized for his relative inexperience, looking like a school-kid who'd shown up to a recital naked and unprepared.

"That's alright. When I said anyone with any experience, I meant it," Sanchez said before dismissing him. The young man left the room like it was on fire.

The second candidate, a junior lieutenant diving specialist named Esmee Kim, who had played the oboe in the U.S. Naval Academy band, was more promising. She was a small, serious woman who worked in the science lab. She eyed the bone flute with interest as Captain Sanchez unlatched its case.

"It's fifty thousand years old, so please be careful," Eva said, trying to keep an edge out of her voice. She always panicked when another person handled an artifact she considered *hers*.

"Rear Admiral Ash said you were keeping it in a tube sock in a dirty backpack," Captain Sanchez murmured. Eva was forced to concede the point.

"Thus far, it has been quite sturdy," she said, daring Junior Lieutenant Kim to contradict her.

"Can you play it?" Captain Sanchez asked, looking at her officer. Eva thought about the people who had died retrieving the flute and felt the need to put a stop to the proceedings.

"No. It's too risky," Eva said. "Most of the people on the team that found it are dead."

"They're all dead," the captain said quietly. Eva looked at her.

"What?"

"Doctor Martin died a week ago en route to the hospital in Manaus."

Eva felt sick. She might have hated the rainforest, but she had enjoyed meeting Dr. Martin, and now he was dead, leaving his goth son to grieve.

"You look perfectly healthy, Dr. Ward," Sanchez said, military steel in her voice. "So I'll ask you again, Lieutenant. Can you play the flute?"

Kim, who already had excellent posture, straightened even further and gave a snappy salute.

"Yes, ma'am," she said. Eva hated asking this young person to take on such a huge risk. Kim had doubtless understood there would be risks associated with joining the military, but Eva guessed dying in the service of experimental xeno-musicology was above and beyond what she'd expected.

Then again, Eva had improved the closer she got to this place.

To her credit, when Junior Lieutenant Kim picked up the flute, her hands never shook.

WHEN FLINT WAS A sophomore in college, his roommate had taken up the electric bass. The endeavor lasted two weeks, which for Flint was two weeks too long. Tuneless twanging had haunted his every waking hour until his roommate lost interest and took up cycling instead. He'd had a special fondness for bicycles ever since.

As it turned out, amateur bass had nothing on the ear-splitting whine that came out of the flute as Kim began experimenting with the instrument's sonic capabilities. The sounds it made were high-pitched and bone-vibrating, eerie notes straight out of a Halloween sound effects cassette tape.

Kim was conscientious, working through various fingerings, experimenting with embouchure and airspeed. After a few hours of earsplitting torture, Rear Admiral Ash sent down ear protection and a specialist physician who poked and prodded at Kim when Kim wasn't busy poking and prodding at the flute.

TWO DAYS LATER, FLINT was feeling relaxed. Seeing Kim lurking in his doorway, he realized why. He wasn't hearing the horrible noise.

"Can I help you, Lieutenant?" he asked. He had tried learning the names of the Hab personnel, but he had found them to be allergic to being called by anything but their ranks.

"I have a hypothesis," Kim said. Flint nodded.

"I know the feeling. What's kicking around up there?" he said, tapping his own forehead as an example.

"It's... I'm not sure Ash will like it."

"So you've come to try it on with me."

The young woman smiled. "I think the flute is just that...a flute."

Flint waited for the punchline.

"But I don't think it was built to be played by a human being," Kim continued, her voice barely audible above the mechanical whine of the Hab's life support systems.

She held out a piece of paper, looking so young and vulnerable that when Flint looked at it, he half expected it to say, "Do you like me, Y/N?" Instead, he found a branching stick figure.

"What is this?" he asked.

"I made a sketch of the structure," Kim said and took a deep breath. "A rough guess at what the...organism the flute was designed for might have looked like."

Flint sighed.

"You think I'm crazy," Kim said.

"I don't think you're crazy. I think we have to call S.A.U.C.E.R."

CHAPTER 25

When Adams arrived in the Hab, he was shaking with so much excitement Flint doubted the man could hold a cup of coffee without spilling half of it on his shoes. He seized Kim's sketch like it was a holy grail, holding it two inches in front of his face for a full minute. She walked him through her reasoning, showing him two holes she thought were meant to be operated by a sort of double-jointed thumb.

"So you *can't* play it," Flint said over Adams's shoulder.

"As is, not really. Not more than what I've been doing. But not just because of the fingerings. I suspect the organism that played this had a different lung capacity and mouth shape."

"We might not even be talking about lungs," Adams said. When Flint cocked an eyebrow at him, he explained himself. "Human beings breathe in and out as our way of obtaining oxygen. But a different organism might have a different reason to take in or expel gases. They might take in air like we take in water."

"In one end and out the other?" Flint said.

"Basically, yes."

"Ah, this organism might have been playing this thing with its own farts?" Somewhere in the room, a tech snorted.

"Have you considered it's not designed to be played in air?" Adams asked, looking at the flute. "Have you tried other gasses? Helium or whatever?"

"Junior Lieutenant Kim is our only instrumentalist at this point, and despite her dedication to this project, she still needs air to survive," Flint said.

"Considering biological constraints, I may have taken this thing as far as it can go," Kim said.

Flint nodded. "We need to build a blower, I think. Some kind of chamber, with a mockup alien hand using Kim's sketches."

The moment the word "alien" left his lips, he regretted it. They had all been calling it the organism.

Captain Sanchez nodded. "I'll call Ash. Get our best tinkerers on it."

"No," Flint said. "Whoever the Navy has won't be as good as Bill."

If Flint was out of place down in the Hab, Bill looked like he had traveled through time. With his bushy beard and handmade clothes (sewn based on the principle that anyone else would cut corners) and overgrown beard, he squeezed out of the airlock like toothpaste through a tube, pulling a large duffel behind him with a clatter.

"Show me to the woodwind section!" he said and walked after a disoriented-looking sailor with a spring in his step.

Knowing Bill, Flint begged some baked goods off the cook a few hours later and headed to a small room where a few of the junior crew had been evicted from their quarters to make room for a workshop. Bill didn't look up but, hearing Flint's footsteps behind him, held out a hand. When Flint placed a donut in it, he finally turned around.

"Can you manufacture it?" he said. Bill munched.

"Sure. The human hand is mechanically non-mysterious. Aliens can't be much different. The bigger question is, should I make it? You told me what you saw in the *Bethany Rose*. I read a little of the mad captain's diary, too. Need me to tell you a story about a little lady named Pandora?"

Flint glanced toward one of the bulkheads, thinking about the huge dome beneath the ice that had been under his feet for so many years.

"I don't know what to tell you, Bill. It's on my ice. Even if it's a can of worms, I've gotta see those worms."

Spoken like a conspiracist, locked in a basement with a lot of red string. But he meant it. Since the first time he'd seen the door, Flint knew he had to open it.

"What do you think is in there?" Flint asked.

"I have a human brain. How could I possibly understand the civilization or motivations of an alien?"

Flint, feeling uncomfortable, left the conversation there. "I need some shut-eye, breakfast is at 1700 hours." Flint left the wizard in peace to tend to his craftsmanship.

THE LIGHTING IN THE Hab was a dim but ever-present glow. Even when Flint turned off the overhead fluorescent light in his quarters, greenish beams filtered into the room under his door, illuminating the small space. So, as he lay in his bunk after a long day playing gopher for Bill, he was disconcerted when the room went pitch black. This darkness was accompanied by a moment of tomblike silence. In a few seconds, Flint realized why it was so unsettling.

The life support systems. They're off.

Bill rustled in the cot beside him. Flint heard him sit up.

"Something's wrong," Bill said. As if he were an oracle, a bright red light clicked on above the door, and a siren screeched to life.

"That can't be good," Flint murmured, and they both sprang up.

Pushing out into the narrow hallway, Flint managed to stop a young sailor who almost barreled through him on her way to some critical task.

"What's going on?" he asked.

"Computers are down," she said, pulling away from him and heading into the hall. "We're switching the life support systems to our analog backups," she shouted over her shoulder.

"Shit," Bill said. "You listen to the safety briefing?"

"Sort of," Flint said. He didn't bother to return the question. The big man's casual demeanor concealed deep wells of paranoia and disaster preparedness. Even as they spoke, Bill was pulling a small oxygen tank and mask from a cubby on the wall. He handed it to Flint and then grabbed one for himself. Flint took it, trying to remember the information a tech had hustled him through when he'd first gotten down here.

"We've got to go get Eva."

WHEN THE LIGHTS WENT off, Eva, who missed her chamomile silk eye mask, thought she might be able to get some sleep. When the alarm sounded a moment later, she put a pillow over her head and lay in bed feeling irate until she heard her door open, and someone yanked the pillow off her face. Bill, standing over her with a look of deep disappointment, thrust a small oxygen tank at her.

"I'm trying to sleep," she said, feeling put upon. When she went to pull her tablet out from the door under her bed, she found the screen blank. Rubbing her eyes, she stared at the two older men.

"All the electronics are out," Flint said.

"Isn't life support running on electronics?" Eva asked, looking with renewed interest at the oxygen bottle in her hands.

"Let's go check on the artifact," Flint said, the flicking warning light casting deep shadows on his craggy face.

Eva, who had spent most of her time in the Hab thinking about the dataset she'd had to abandon at Gucci's, clambered to her feet. All she'd done since coming down here was consume more than her fair share of oxygen. As they approached the workshop, she had a sinking feeling.

The artifact was gone, along with Bill's artificial blow chamber and hand. Eva sucked in her breath, fighting the urge to hyperventilate. *Try not to waste even more oxygen.* She didn't think she deserved much, given her critical failure at the key archaeological skill of *not* losing ancient valuable artifacts.

"Maybe security scooped it up when the alarms went off," Eva said.

"The only security down here is the million pounds of water bearing down on us," Flint said.

Eva thought about where she was. "If whoever took it wants to play hide and seek, that's fine, but they can't exactly go anywhere."

"Not unless they're working with an outsider and cut the life support as a distraction," Bill murmured. The three of them looked at each other, then turned and sprinted toward the docking bay.

When they arrived, they found Junior Lieutenant Kim standing near the airlock, looking terrified.

"Kim?"

As Eva heard Flint's voice, she realized Kim wasn't alone. A small figure stepped out from behind her, fist clenched around the toolbox where they'd been keeping Bill's mechanical hand. It was Jake Adams. Alien expert and traitor, a flickering gleam in his eyes from more than just the emergency lights.

"Everything okay, Doctor?" Flint said, his motions slowing to a standstill as they saw what was in Adams's other hand.

A pistol.

"Everyone came to my party. I'm honored."

"Give me back my flute!" Eva said, feeling impetuous and annoyed. There was little in life she hated more than being woken up unexpectedly.

Adams snorted, his lip curling up in disgust. As Eva stared at him, she noticed an oxygen mask hanging limp around his neck.

"You can put a stop to this now, Adams," Flint said, the vivacity drained from his voice. "Think about how this ends for you. You can't take the *Devilfish*. Even if you can steer it, what then? You're smack dab under one of the biggest warships of the world's most powerful military. They'll come after you."

"Maybe. If they can get their electronics or communications back online. Although to be honest, I didn't expect to be dealing with so many people who were still breathing."

He tapped his oxygen mask. "This tuna can must have been retrofitted with analog backups after we got hold of the blueprints during our planning phase. Shows you what I get for going to the trouble of buying the world's most powerful EMP. I bet they're having fun up top."

"What's your plan? An electromagnetic pulse to knock out the electricity? What do I look like, a Radio Shack nerd?" Eva asked. "Fence the flute to some billionaire alien enthusiast? If you can find one who believes you?"

Adams snorted again. "You think so little of me. Just like the Navy. I can't blame you for your lack of imagination. If you were in my shoes, I'm sure you'd go right to petty theft. In fact, I have loftier goals. After all...there's only one reason to steal a key."

The airlock opened behind him.

"Let the lieutenant go," Bill said. Eva winced. She hadn't heard him sound even a little annoyed. Now, his voice rumbled with fury.

"No can do, mountain man. Somebody has to toot the horn."

Eva looked at Kim, who was clearly afraid, although keeping her cool. She thought about everything she'd been through over the past few weeks. Feeling a little foolish, she shouted toward Adams.

"Take me instead! I've been with the artifact for weeks. I have information about it even the Navy doesn't know."

She thought about the data on the thumb drive.

Adams whistled. "Holding out on the admiral? Now *that* I can respect. Sure. Why not? It's your funeral at sea."

He pushed Kim away, and Eva walked toward the airlock, feeling a magnetic pull. What was she doing? Risking her life. For what?

Still, the motion of her feet increased, pulling her into the submersible. What was happening to her?

I have to get inside that dome.

She didn't know why, but she knew it was true.

CHAPTER 26

FLINT WAS FURIOUS. HE shouldn't have let Eva go out into the cold ocean with that creepy little S.AU.C.E.R. freak.

She's going to get inside the dome before I do.

Adams might not have killed their life support as he'd intended, but he had cut them off from the outside world. The Hab's screens were dark, and its comms were cold.

Flint stood in the docking bay for a minute, marinating in the sudden cessation of activity.

"We let him take the flute," he said, disconsolate.

Kim, a few feet away, cleared her throat.

"No, sir, we didn't. He took the copy I made in the 3D printer so we could test Bill's hand."

Flint almost never saw Bill surprised, but now the big man's jaw dropped a fraction of an inch.

"Well shit," he said. "That's good, right?"

Flint wasn't so sure. "It means we let Eva go out with a little creep who's about to be very, very angry. Hm. Where's the flute?"

"Locked up in Captain Sanchez's quarters. I had a gut feeling," Kim said.

"Some feeling," Bill said.

"Yeah," Flint agreed. "Let us know if you have another one."

For the first time in weeks, Eva thought about her daughter. It wasn't because she didn't care. The thoughts were always there, but they were an underground river. Even though she was on the other side of the Earth, Sophie was in the same time zone, a quirk of longitude. Although from the bottom of the ocean Eva had no instinctual idea what time it was.

She wondered if Sophie would be better or worse off without her. Raised by Steve, she would probably grow up to be hopelessly unambitious—a professional hacky sacker or wedding deejay. Shuddering at this thought, Eva vowed to live. Her eyes scanned to assess her surroundings. She watched Adams fiddle with a series of dials and knobs.

"If you fried everything, how come the sub still runs?" she asked.

"Manual backup," he muttered. The knuckles of his hands were white, and a small muscle at the corner of his jaw twitched.

"How does she handle?" Eva asked, arching an eyebrow as he struggled. Adams responded with a non-committal grunt and then swore as the sub surged forward.

"What's your endgame here?" she asked.

"The truth," Adams grunted. Eva blinked in surprise. "It might be hard for someone who sees antiquities as interchangeable stacks of cash to understand."

Eva tried to feel offended, but this was a more-or-less accurate assessment of her career.

"Explain it to me," she said. Maybe she could find a hole in the conversation that would let her worm her way into his psyche and put a stop to his insanity.

The sub lurched again, and Adams sighed.

"You remember the Topojunga fire?"

She'd seen photos. Hillsides of houses, glowing orange, blackened frames falling to ash.

"What was that, five years ago?"

"Six years, three months, four days. There was a historic drought in California that year, and the reservoir the fire trucks needed was dust. My wife and two sons were blocked in by the fire on both sides."

Eva's throat closed.

"My wife told me she wanted her ashes scattered in our garden. There was never a body, but I guess she got her wish." His back was to her as he spoke, shoulders tight and hunched. "The Earth is dying, Doctor Ward. We're just seeing the first wave now. Fires, tornadoes, and the only species capable of seeing what's really going on has shut its eyes. If humanity has a future, that future is extraterrestrial."

Metal scraped on metal somewhere below them, and Adams swore.

"So you've given up on humanity and decided to throw your lot in with the little green men?"

"Mankind doesn't have what it takes. If there's a chance of connecting with a species that does, it's a chance I want to take. I'm going inside the dome, Doctor Ward."

"Whatever's in there might be a lot worse than a wildfire," Eva said.

"From my perspective, that's literally impossible," Adams replied. After a moment, she heard the crackle of a walkie-talkie.

"I thought all comms were down?"

"They are. Unless you stuck a few walkies and an underwater comms buoy in a Faraday suitcase. Which I did."

He pushed a button.

"Hey. I've got the flute. And a little surprise for you," Adams said.

"I'm intrigued," a voice replied. It was too distorted to identify, but something about it was familiar. Eva's stomach lurched. Adams's walkie crackled again. "See you soon. Over and out."

CHAPTER 27

"There's nothing we can do until we reestablish comms," Captain Sanchez said, her hand resting on the flute's case. Flint tried to pay attention to her tone and face, but he couldn't stop staring at the box. He growled under his breath.

"How long will that take?" he said.

"I won't know until we reestablish comms," the captain said with aggravated irony. Flint felt like breaking something. He looked around the room, but everything in his immediate eyeline was bolted down. The captain tapped her fingers on the case. "The EMP can't have fried equipment beyond, say, a one-mile radius. The Navy doubtlessly has resources zooming toward our location as we speak."

"Eva's out in the middle of the ocean with the enemy. You can't just leave her there."

"Doctor Ward is not mission critical," the captain said, more matter-of-fact than cruel. She sounded annoyed they were still talking; he guessed she was used to being obeyed without discussion. Flint sighed.

"Please let me know the second you hear something," he said. "I'll be in my room."

He made a show of storming out, and turned left toward the hallway that led to his room. Instead of going there, however, he looped through the mess hall and circled back, slipping into one of the narrow toilet stalls along the corridor outside the captain's quarters. He usually avoided this toilet because there was a gap along the hinges that made a chunk of the stall, and so the hallway, visible. Including the captain's door. He waited there, inside the head, as a series of subordinates went in and out of the quarters, low murmurs about radio waves, satellite reception, and air supply filtering into the cramped room. His spirits rose as he saw a sailor bring a large carafe of coffee from the mess.

Twenty minutes later, Sanchez exited her quarters and strode across the hallway. He pulled back as he saw her peer into the occupied stall, then go into the one next to it.

This was his chance. Flint slipped out, moving as quickly as his joints would let him, and prayed she hadn't locked the door behind her.

She hadn't.

Flint considered taking the entire case. There was a rough road ahead of them, and it would be useful for protecting the flute. Sighing, he decided against it. If the captain hadn't locked her door, he doubted she would check to see if someone had stolen the artifact while she was in the head.

Flint had seen the flute many times as Junior Ensign Kim worked with it, but he had never handled it. As he flipped open the latches of the case, the bone-like material shone white. When he touched it, he was filled with a sense of purpose so solid it frightened him. Suddenly, it was there in the room with him, tangible. He had to go to the dome. The last time he had been this certain about anything was twenty years ago when he'd paid four hundred dollars for a long-distance call to tell his wife he was leaving her and staying in Antarctica.

I'll get inside. I have to.

The words felt embedded in his consciousness as if they had physical weight. But something was missing. What was it? A vague secondary purpose returned to him.

I'm not going to lose someone on my watch! I'm going to save Eva, and I'm going inside that dome.

Leaving the captain's quarters, he headed down to the *Devilfish* bay to wait.

THEY HAD ONLY BEEN in the water twenty minutes when Adams cut the engine of the *Devilfish*.

"I thought we were going to the dome," Eva said.

"We're waiting for our ride," Adams said, his face sour and unresponsive. The porthole that looked out into Weddell Ocean was an unchanging aquamarine circle, and after a few minutes, she stopped looking at it.

"You know, I have a daughter," she said, pushing her words into the thick silence. A brief and terrifying fury passed over Adams's face, and Eva felt frightened. She had meant to arouse his empathy, not anger. *It's like telling a starving man you're going to a buffet.* Adams coughed and smiled a thin smile.

"When you meet my partner, you're going to be surprised. A little reunion, if you will," he said. Thinking about the voice on the other end of the walkie, Eva shivered. She was pretty sure it had been a man. Raising a curious eyebrow, Eva searched Adams's face for information. His smile widened, but if he had anything else to say, he kept it to himself.

After several minutes, a dark shape crossed the porthole, followed by a decisive thump of metal on metal.

As Adams busied himself with knobs and dials, Eva had a sudden terror he might screw up the docking procedure, flooding the small capsule with ice-cold water that would freeze her lungs from the inside while she drowned.

"Do you know what you're doing?" she said, starting to hyperventilate and wondering how much oxygen they even had in there.

"If you think you can do better, Doctor Ward, by all means, start pushing buttons," Adams muttered.

Her breathing slowed, but she found herself unable to look away from the porthole until Adams spun the hatch open, and she saw air on the other side.

Not just air. Eva's jaw dropped as she saw the ruddy face of the man clambering through the porthole.

It was Sigmund Wulf. He was nothing much to look at in a photograph, slightly shorter than her with red-brown hair and a barrel chest. Although he usually wore cowboy boots to make himself seem taller. His eyes were the same, though, glittering with life, and his rich voice had a careless confidence that was immensely attractive. In black fatigues, he looked treacherous.

It made Eva feel sick. Wulf's eyes sparkled as he watched her shocked expression. He had always loved to see her off balance.

She considered slapping him, but there was so little room in the *Devilfish* the gesture would be more pathetic than satisfying, an inert push of the palm against skin.

She settled for glaring at him with an open and unforced disgust.

"Evie!" he said, wrapping his big arms around her. Half a mile underwater, and he still smelled amazing. She hated him for it.

"I thought you were dead," she said.

"Sorry to disappoint."

"Don't be. I got enormous pleasure out of it. Almost as much as I'll feel when I kill you myself."

"Ever the firebrand," Wulf chuckled, turning to Adams. "Good on you for not sinking this thing. I'd given it a fifty-fifty chance." Smiling, he chucked Adams on the shoulder. "You know, Evie was one of my best students until I found her pocketing Roman coins at a dig site. She fenced a baker's dozen before I figured it out. Very impressive. Plenty of graduate students are tempted to steal, but few have the spunk to make the right criminal connections."

Eva felt her jaw clench shut. Things had been so tight that semester, and they had dug up so many Roman coins. Professionally, it was a low moment for her, made even worse by how Wulf had responded, which was to threaten to turn her in unless she wrote his papers and did all his grading for him. The papers, anyway, had made her a better archaeologist. And eventually, she learned the truth.

"You only found out because you were using the same fence for the same coins," she said. She'd considered turning him in, but by that point, it felt like mutually assured destruction.

"Great minds," Wulf agreed. "Come on, Eves, don't look at me like that. We had a great time in Rome. Remember that little spaghetti place below the faculty housing?"

His hand grazed her left butt cheek, and as she slowed her breathing, she imagined the places she hoped to someday put that hand. Like a steaming mug of nuclear waste or the mouth of a Komodo dragon.

"Aren't you going to ask me how I faked my death?" Wulf said, a self-satisfied grin spreading across his face.

"I can tell you're desperate to share, so no," Eva said, turning to stare out the useless porthole.

Wulf's grin pulled wider, and he tapped a white canine.

"I used my real teeth. Had 'em knocked out and replaced with veneers. Can't recommend it enough. I could chew through a boot now."

"Care to demonstrate?" Eva said.

Wulf shrugged. "No time. We have an alien dome to infiltrate."

Eva pressed her mouth closed. She wasn't thrilled about the circumstances, but she had to admit she felt a pull. The dome loomed somewhere in the underwater distance, awaiting their entrance, creme brulee waiting to be cracked.

"It's going to be a tight squeeze," Wulf said. "But you'll be okay. It's about the same size as that storage closet down the hall from my office, which I don't remember you complaining about."

Eva was gratified to see Adams roll his eyes.

"Ladies first."

THE DIVING SUITS THE Navy used at these depths were practically small submersibles with sleek, aerodynamic helmets, Teflon fabric, and internal heating mechanisms. The seals and latches looked straightforward enough, although Flint realized he wouldn't know if he'd gotten the details right until it was too late. He stared at the curve of the helmets. The dome was waiting.

In spite of the crisis, the Hab was quieter than he'd ever heard it. Severed from the outside world, most normal duties were suspended, and the crew were using the lull to catch up on sleep. *Smart,* Flint thought as he pulled the clear bell of a helmet over his head.

It took him a moment to realize what was bothering him.

His hands. They weren't hurting at all. He waggled his fingers in a wave, a gesture that normally pinched a nerve and made the corner of his eye twitch. He felt the rubber diving gloves against his skin, but otherwise, nothing.

He closed two latches of the helmet. Staring at the rubberized gloves over his hands, he began to wonder how he was going to operate the controls to the moon pool when he heard a noise in the room.

He remained motionless, hoping whoever had come in wouldn't notice there was a person in the suit.

This was fruitless, as moments later, a face appeared in the transparent window of the helmet.

"Flint?" the voice said.

It was Lieutenant Kim. Flint felt the air leave his body. He couldn't run. The jig was up. Ash might not have him court-martialed, but he didn't think treason charges were out of the question.

Kim stared at him, looked around, and lowered her voice.

"You have the flute."

Flint nodded, a brief lowering of his chin. He held out a rubber-clad hand. The ensign looked down and nodded, then reached for the clasps on his helmet. He waited for her to remove it and call the captain.

Instead, a moment later, her hands pulled away, and she nodded in satisfaction.

"The seals look good. Do you have any idea what you're doing?"

Flint had been scuba diving once, on his honeymoon, and the experience had left him with a burning hatred of the tropics.

"No," he admitted.

Kim nodded. "I'm coming with you," she said. "You need someone to play the flute."

She took it from him, then, and with quick movements, began putting on one of the other diving suits in the room. Flint was shocked.

"Are you sure?"

"I could tell it wasn't with the captain. I felt it. I followed that impulse to this room. It's time, Flint. If we go now, we'll be able to get into the dome. We have to get in. I have a gut feeling."

"What's your plan to play the flute?" he asked her.

She tapped the backup air supply hose hanging from his suit. "Detach the extra air and run it through the mouthpiece. The gloves should have just enough flexibility. We won't be able to communicate underwater, though. The radios in the suits fried with everything else."

Before she finished putting on her own suit, she told him what they would do.

THE VESSEL THAT HAD met up with the *Devilfish* was less of a ship and more of a titanium alloy tube with some light steering capabilities. They were going into a tunnel, so she supposed it made sense. As Eva crawled over to a shallow well in the back she guessed was meant to be a seat, she felt the weight of the ocean press in on her.

"How are you p this?" she asked. "I didn't think submarine money was one of the perks of tenure. Which being dead, you no longer have."

Wulf, pressing against her more than he had to as he crawled into the seat next to her, shrugged and smiled a mischievous smile.

"You must have fenced a lot of Roman coins," she muttered.

She could see the sub's monitor from her seat, and half an hour later, watched the 3D wireframe graphics as they approached the lava tube that would take them into the mass of rock under the Antarctica surface. Eva, who hated being in tight spaces, dredged up a breathing exercise she hadn't had to use since she'd worked with some petroglyphs in a cave in France. Four in, five out. The touch of claustrophobia that made her take the stairs if she was going more than three floors hit her here, squeezed into a tube inside a cave. The wireframe model of the tunnel became hypnotic, white lines out of a vapor-wave music video moving inexorably toward them. Wulf's hand grazed her thigh, and she slapped it away.

"You'll be okay. Just keep breathing," he said, watching her. He'd been on that French dig the first time she'd had a claustrophobic panic attack. After that, he'd recommended her for every cave, tunnel, or crypt-related project he could. The bastard.

Fear was distorting the environment around her, making the lights brighter. It was hard to focus, but she managed to glance at Wulf's face long enough to realize he was enjoying watching her like this.

"Just another minute," Adams said. "Why don't you prep the woodwind section?"

He handed the flute back to Wulf.

"I admit, I'm excited to get my mitts on it," Wulf said, opening the latches. There was deep silence for a moment as he stared inside the case.

He looked at Eva with a depth of hatred she recognized from when he'd backhanded her in the car on their way home from a party where she'd pointed out some factual inaccuracies in his assessment of a host's Ming vase.

She couldn't help it. Looking at the flute, she flinched back.

It was wrong. She had to hand it to the Navy's manufacturing capabilities; it looked pretty good. But this flute was a dull gray, some kind of sturdy, synthetic plastic, not the glistening bone material of the real flute.

"They made a copy. I didn't know," Eva said.

"We're not going to get inside an alien dome with a cheap hunk of plastic!" Wulf screamed, his voice oppressive in the small space. Eva looked around for something to defend herself with. Wulf barely had enough room to hit her, but she thought he might try.

"Maybe it will still work," she said.

Adams had turned around to face them both.

"If Kim was using this for testing, they must have pretty similar sonic qualities. Right? By the time we can call the ship and ask them to swim over with the original, they'll be sending us gift-wrapped torpedoes. The dummy flute will have to work." Desperation clawed its way through Adams's voice.

Eva glanced at the monitor.

They were at the door.

CHAPTER 28

EVEN WITH INTERNAL HEATING, Flint bit his tongue in pain as the icy Antarctica waters surrounded the suit. He remembered this was how they tested new painkillers. They submerged their subjects' hands in ice water. The heating in the suit would keep the edge off the agony, but it would not be a fun swim.

Kim looked at him through her helmet and curled her hand into their agreed-upon signal.

He was still in control of his actions. Sort of. If he wanted to blink, or move his arm, he could. But in moments where his attention lagged, a powerful backup process took over, puppeteering his body through smooth, specific actions.

He saw Kim press the buttons on a submerged control panel, and the outer bay opened below them.

There was a mechanical noise and the water lock closed. A moment later, an identical noise sounded. Flint peered into the darkness. It was useless. There was only room on the suits for so many flares. Kim said they should use the guideline out to the drilling machinery and save the flares for later.

Normally, the divers working from the Hab used small submersible rovers to travel around. But they had gone haywire in the EMP burst. They were stuck with fins. Kim had barely managed to attach them to the suits, which had not been encouraging.

There were small emergency lights around the edge of the outer bay, a dim ring that emptied out into utter darkness. Swimming after Kim to the guideline, he began to pull himself away from the glow and into the pitch-black ocean.

The weight of the ocean around him was intense, and the silence was complete. At least, he knew, it was too cold for sharks. Not for orcas, though. He wondered how much he looked like a delicious seal.

Flint kicked his feet, pulling himself along the line and wishing he could talk to Kim. In almost no time at all, his thighs were burning. He patted the flares in his pocket, resisting the urge to pull one out and illuminate the surrounding environment. Probably he wouldn't see anything. Probably, but not certainly. As the marine biology teams at the station loved to say, they hadn't discovered a tenth of what was down here. And a lot of what they had discovered was weird. He'd take rocks over a giant squid any day of the week.

This must be what death is like. Floating in the endless cold darkness.

No, death would be better than this because he wouldn't have to be there for it.

He couldn't see or hear anything, and he quickly grew used to the smell of his own breath. Much longer without any stimulus, and he would start to hallucinate. Or maybe not. Maybe the pain of the cold would pin him to reality.

Flint's world shrank to the movement of his legs and the feeling of his hands around the rope. Kick, kick, pull. Kick, kick, pull. Kick, kick, pull. It was purgatorial, almost lulling. Some endless interlude later, he was caught off guard when a dark shape slammed into his body. Sputtering and clawing at it with his arms, he felt it move.

THE SLIM SUBMERSIBLE HAD speakers, and Adams busied himself with setting up Bill's mechanical hand and blower in the bow of the boat.

"This is excellent work," he said, testing the double joint on the mechanical thumb.

Eva wrapped her arms around her knees and watched, feeling like she was falling into a bottomless pit. Something very wrong was about to happen. She was sure of it. She glanced at Wulf, who had turned his aggravation on Adams instead of her.

A single, clear thought appeared in her head like a transparent glass ball. She had to stop this. They were on a track barreling toward burning oil, and someone had to pull the brakes. She looked at Adams, then down at the blower.

"You haven't set it up correctly," she said, hoping the lie wasn't too obvious.

"Yes, I have," Adams said, looking up at her. The expression on his face was less confident.

Eva crawled toward him, feeling her window to avert catastrophe closing.

"Let me show you," she said, using an imperious voice she reserved for rich people at auctions.

She reached into the blower box, smiled at Adams, gripped the mechanical hand as if she were shaking it, and *pulled.*

It came out of the box with almost no effort, only a faint crackle and pop from the wires.

"What the fuck did you do?" Adams shouted as he realized she was holding the hand in her own.

"You stupid bitch," she heard from behind her, and a hand pulled her ankle toward the stern of the sub. As Eva yelped in pain, Adams ripped the hand away from her and pushed her back.

"You can't do this! Something horrible is going to happen if you play that thing!" Eva said.

Adams leveled his gun at her face. The gun. Shit. She'd almost forgotten about it.

"Well, lucky for you, I'm not going to be playing it. You are," Adams said.

"I won't do it," Eva said. "There's something wrong. And you can't risk shooting me. You'll collapse the sub."

"One way or another, this dome is the end of the road for me," Adams said. "So, you're going to play that flute. If you don't, I'm going to shoot you and take my chances with the ocean. Before I shoot you, however, I'm going to contact a friend and have him visit your daughter. Sophie? It's a dangerous world for a kid these days. The people on our side aren't sickos, but they have enough money to hire a few if they need to."

Eva sucked in her breath. Shit.

Adams retrieved the flute from its box.

"I barely understand how to play it," Eva stammered.

"Then I hope you're a quick study."

CHAPTER 29

FLINT SCREAMED IN FEAR, thoughts of leviathans and tentacular monstrosities flooding his limbic system. After a moment, however, nothing happened, and he realized he had smacked into Kim.

They were at the drill rig.

Back in the moon pool bay, she'd told him the drill rig was about fifty meters from the entrance to the lava tube. They'd need to swim across the open ocean and use the flares to locate it. He tapped his belt, the small cylinders smooth under his rubber-coated fingers.

The darkness was suddenly illuminated with a red glow. The metal structure of the drill rig appeared beside them, stretching along the rock face.

Flint took a deep breath and let go of the guideline. This was it. If they didn't find the tube before they ran out of flares, he would spend the last hours of his life freezing in the dark, waiting for his oxygen to run out.

They had agreed to use one flare at a time. Kim would light hers first. Then Flint. They would alternate until they found the tube.

Flint saw Kim look back to make sure he was still there, then followed her as she began to kick her way across the open ocean toward the massive shelf of rock and ice in the distance.

When the flare ran out, Flint felt a wave of panic so strong he almost forgot the plan. Pulling the guideline in the dark had been frightening. Being in the open ocean in the dark was unbearable, and his limbs flailed until he forced himself to calm down. It was his turn to light a flare. He wrapped his glove around one of the cylinders, pulled it from his belt, removed the cap, and dropped it. Guilt washed through him as he watched the tiny tube float down into the abyss, a departing flicker of light. Before it disappeared, he thought he saw something with an undulating body swimming through it.

Cursing at himself for further thinning their already anorexic margin of error, Flint grasped at his waist. As he lit the flare, he gripped it so tightly he felt a twinge of pain in his fingers.

A second flare lit up ten feet away from him. Shit. As he'd fumbled in the darkness, Kim had also lit one. Through the window of her helmet, he saw the look of alarm on her face, illuminated by the red glow of the tubes.

Two flares are wasted now. She pointed at herself, then gestured at a point high along the rock shelf. Then pointed at him and gestured low.

Divide and conquer while we have two lights going.

He swam low.

The rock escarpment was uneven, and while the drill hole was large, they had so little light they wouldn't be able to see it until they were right on top of it. Twenty feet away from the wall, he swam on, alert to ledges that could conceal the entrance to the tunnel.

When his flare went out several minutes later, he swore.

Whose turn is it?

After sitting a minute in darkness, he decided it must be his, and lit another flare, only to curse as a matching glow appeared above him. They were running through their flares twice as fast as expected. Not to mention the flare he'd dropped. He kept swimming.

When the next flare went out, he vowed to sit in darkness forever if it killed him, and hoped Kim wasn't making the same choice. After an agonizing, cold two minutes, a glow appeared above him, and he swam toward it. As he did, the edge of the red light caught on something on the wall.

The edge of a lava tube disappeared into the darkness. A curving ridge of rock, and beyond it, pitch black nothing.

Flint and Kim kicked into the tube together, alternating their flares.

Two hundred yards in, the tube changed from natural lava into drilled granite.

And then it split.

Flint swore under his breath as he looked at the Y-shaped junction. They had abandoned a test tunnel after the rock formation they were drilling through had proved too unstable and damaged their drill. Forced to backtrack, they had successfully drilled the second tunnel all the way to the alien dome. Now, he couldn't tell which tunnel was which. In the dim red light of the flare, the geology was inscrutable. After so long in the cold, his brain had slowed. He looked down at his compass, but this close to the pole, the needle spun frenetically, pointing toward everything and nothing. He looked at Kim, floating ten feet away from him. They couldn't afford to lose more time.

He went left.

Three hundred yards and two flares later, they hit a blank wall.

He felt along his belt. There were three flare cylinders there. One or two for the trip back, and then...

The dome was another four hundred yards from the junction.

They weren't going to have enough flares.

As he and Kim made eye contact, he watched her come to the same conclusion. Her face was empty of all but a dark resolve, and she turned away from him and started to swim back the way they'd come.

WHEN EVA WRAPPED HER fingers around the shaft of the flute, it felt wrong, like going to shake someone's hand and grasping bleached bone instead.

She would have to try it. She didn't think Adams wanted to kill her or Sophie, but her gut told her he would pull the trigger himself without hesitation if it served his mission. The xenologist made a few final adjustments to the sub's speakers and then pointed toward a small microphone clipped to the dashboard.

"Play into there," Adams said. "The sound will be amplified through the water.

She wished she had the real flute. Remembering how ill Dr. Armand had looked, the instinct confused her. The flute's power was clear and dangerous, even if its mechanism was opaque.

She looked at the big door, imagining the thousands of tiny cilia lining it, waiting to be swayed with a perfect musical key.

"No more stalling. Showtime," Adams said and flipped the mic button to ON.

Eva arranged her fingers on the flute and blew a tentative note. As the sound fell off, the three of them waited in silence, the sub's running lights illuminating the door.

Nothing happened. Adams waved at her to try again. She did, moving her fingers into different places, covering random holes. This time she blew three notes in sequence. The flute emitted an irregular whine, the horrible lovechild of a flute and a kazoo. She dropped the instrument to her side, feeling useless. This was pointless, playing an alien instrument she had never practiced with. She'd probably have more success auditioning for the Metropolitan Opera.

There was a deep rumble. Eva, still concentrating on the flute, assumed Adams had given up and turned the sub around. But the running lights continued to illuminate the cylinder ahead of them. They weren't moving.

No. The sound was coming from the door.

It was hard to tell what was happening at first. The door was thirty feet away, and the lights of the sub, shining through ocean water flecked with microflora and plankton, barely illuminated it.

In the middle of the door, a circle the diameter of a teacup saucer detached from the smooth surface around it and flowed toward them.

Eva had assumed the cilia lining the door were short. Now, she realized they must extend some distance into the dome because those tiny threads came to life, reaching out toward the sub, an immense flexible arm like a fiber optic cable. *Is it trying to dock with us?*

"You were supposed to open it, not call out the guards!" Adams shouted. Was that what was happening? Was the thing coming towards them mechanical or organic? Were they friends or enemies, and could the tube tell the difference?

It looked organic, twisting in the water like an eel, slithering with curved movements toward the ship. Were the aliens friendly? Did the aliens know *they* were friendly? *Were* they friendly? Eyes glued to the porthole, Eva watched as the cable was fifteen feet from the sub. Then ten. Then five.

Then it disappeared. The sudden absence was shocking. Eva strained her eyes, looking through the porthole, trying to see where the tube of cilia had gone.

"Is it behind us?" Wulf asked. Too loud, as always.

Eva stared into the water. The light beams continued to illuminate the open ocean, but something was different. Something about the way the light looked.

She realized what had happened at the same time she heard the noise. The sound was faint and eerie like a million needles tapping at the sub all at once.

The tube hadn't disappeared after all. It had split into thousands of fibers too small to be seen by the naked eye. And now those fibers were wrapping around the ship.

The pins-and-needle *tink tink tink* reverberated, and Eva watched Adams grab the controllers with both hands, toggling switches and pressing buttons. In the battle between flight and fight, the flight had won.

The muscles in Adams's freckled forearms strained as he yanked back.

"Nothing's happening!" he screamed.

The tapping needles grew louder.

The nanofibers are drilling into the ship.

The light shifted, and the air felt dusty. *Am I breathing them?* It would be like breathing cotton candy or fiberglass.

Suddenly, the threads were visible again as the nano-scale materials twisted together into barely visible, undulating threads. They were everywhere now, filling the ship like noodles in boiling water, roiling and twisting. She batted at a coiling nest in front of her face, but more threads filled in behind what she batted away like an ever-expanding cornsilk mass.

They wrapped around her wrists, tearing the plastic flute from her grasp and binding her fingers together. She tried to pull her hands away, but the room was stuffed now. Threads, threads everywhere. She was breathing them, she must be;

there was no way to avoid it. They would stuff her like a teddy bear until she suffocated. Was there any room in the sub for oxygen? How was she still alive? She tried to blink and found there was no room for her eyes to shut, held open by threads she could feel writhe against her eyeballs. She screamed and felt more twist down her throat as it opened.

There was a constriction, then. Not crushing, but tightening, as the teeming mass around her knitted itself together into a solid mat.

Something warm flooded the threads. At first, she panicked, thinking the sub had cracked open and the cold sea was coming to claim her. But this wasn't freezing saltwater. It was a warm gel. As it covered her open eyeballs, it was a relief. It was less of a relief as she felt it flood her lungs, making her gag and sending her muscles into spasms, trying to expel it. Several minutes later, when she still wasn't dead, she realized the gel must be oxygenated. Her heart was still beating, even if the steady rise and fall of her chest had been replaced by a static fullness.

And then she heard a bursting noise and felt herself move. She was being pulled.

CHAPTER 30

BACK ON THE RIGHT path, Kim and Flint swam with careful movements. He felt his own motivation flagging, keeping his eyes on the rough bottom of the tunnel. An idea forming in his mind, he swam toward it, and he grasped the rough stone with his rubber gloves. Closing his eyes, he pulled himself across the rough rock, experimenting with moving through the tunnel blindly.

When he opened his eyes again, he found he'd gotten disoriented and begun to pull himself along the tunnel horizontally. If he kept up his current route, he would send himself in an eternal loop-de-loop, ending every circle where he'd started it. He closed his eyes and tried again, trying to feel differences in texture along the path where the drill bit had cut into the rock. More times than not, sharp angles on the rock chunks pointed in the right direction. If Flint kept feeling for the angles, they'd make it a little farther. Glancing up, understanding dawned on Kim's face for a half second before her flare guttered out.

Flint reached toward the flare at his waist. It would be his last one. He tapped it, then pulled his hand back. He would save it. He would try to carry on without it, and if the situation was dire, he would light it.

The situation IS dire.

He felt for the next angular point along the bottom of the tunnel. Then the next, and the next. If he was being honest with himself, his crawling speed was a tenth or a twentieth of his swimming speed. Still, he continued to pull, hand over hand, in the darkness, the final flare in his pocket easing his mind. Ten minutes passed, or five or an hour, before his hands grew wet and clammy.

Wet. *Why is my hand wet?* He directed his attention toward his limbs and quickly identified the problem. Every so often, a drop of water seeped through the tip of the glove over his left ring finger. In his eagerness to pull himself through the tunnel, against all odds, he had been too rough. In the process of reaching for sharp edges, a pinprick hole had developed in the finger of his diving glove.

Terrified, he pulled his hand away from the rock.

He'd held onto a small comfort while he swam. If he ran out of oxygen, the nitrogen rebreathers in his suit would keep circulating. Nitrogen narcosis was one of the better ways to go, he knew. But now, there was a chance he might drown, cold and trapped in the dark.

Starting to panic, he reached down and pulled the flare from his belt, twisting the cap and lighting it. The glow was calming. For a moment, looking behind him, he thought Kim had abandoned him, refusing to continue without flares. As he spun in a panic, he realized she was ahead of him.

Of course, she's faster than you. She's decades younger and does PT.

As he swam toward her, a line of cold water trickled down his glove onto his forearm, and he shivered. Kim fell in beside him, and together they swam into their last light.

Flint was afraid but tried to pay attention. If this tunnel was the last thing he would ever see, he wanted to *see* it. He looked at the specks glowing red in the water, at the harsh, jagged edges of the rock along the walls of the tunnels, the light casting weird, underwater waves onto the walls. Dying under the ice wasn't so much worse than dying on it.

A thin shape moved in the water in front of him, and he focused his eyes. It was a segmented worm, not much wider than spaghetti, clear and waving in the water. It was at least fifty feet long. The flare illuminated sections of its body as they swam past it.

He looked over at Kim, at her grim face beneath her visor. The light of the flare turned her eyes red for a moment. And then it went out.

Flint floated, listless, sending out a silent thanks to the segmented worm for offering *something* to look at. Pinpricks of fear danced up his spine and he became aware that if he stopped moving, the sensation would be agony.

He swam in the dark, the kicking of his feet taking on a meditative quality. Would Kim keep swimming? He hoped so. Fear jolted into him several moments later as he heard the loud bang of metal on rock. Then, he screeched to a halt as the face of his helmet hit the side of the tunnel. The bang he heard must have been Kim hitting the wall.

She was still swimming.

Flint moved more slowly now, hands in front of him, not wanting the horrible jolt of hitting rock.

When he began to hallucinate, it was a relief. Looking at the dancing lights in the distance, he felt grateful for the quirk of neurochemistry that refused to leave him floating in the dark. Who was he to refuse his brain's closing performance? He swam toward the light.

Feeling unhinged, he wondered what else his mind would conjure. The marine biologist he'd fallen in love with a decade ago, who had gone back to her husband and kids when her research term had ended? Or something more esoteric, a neon-fueled laser-light kaleidoscope?

He was disappointed when the lights never changed. They just glowed, soft yellow, getting closer and closer.

As he kicked his left fin, something grabbed it. He kicked back, like a horse, instinctually, and then turned and saw it was Kim.

How can I see her?

She pointed toward the light. *She can see it, too.*

Flint's whole forearm was wet and cold, and the arthritis that had abandoned him came back with full force, burning his nerves with icy fire.

The pain shocked him back to reality. He stared at the lights. Then at Kim, barely visible through the water.

It wasn't a hallucination. It was a vessel. As they swam toward it, Flint wondered if it was the *Devilfish*. But no, this sub was smaller, with a sleek torpedo shape. Or at least, it had been before something the size of a great white shark had ripped a hole in the side six feet across. Flint peered inside the flooded chamber as they reached it.

What could punch through a sub like this? He looked around for clues, but there was nothing. Just the hole.

And there was no one there. As he approached, Flint had expected to find frozen bodies. But there was nothing, just empty water and running lights pointed straight at the alien door.

The door! Flint looked at Kim and saw her eyes gleam with hope. He watched as she swam toward it.

Ten feet away, she pulled the flute from a holster at her waist and positioned the emergency air tube at its opening. Bubbles floated through the water as she released the air and then formed a seal around the opening with her fingers, forcing the emergency oxygen supply through the flute.

Nothing happened.

The pressure isn't high enough. Unlike their helmets, the emergency air hose wasn't designed for these depths, and with the huge weight of water above them, there wasn't enough pressure to play the flute.

Kim tried again and again, for minutes, until Flint felt so tense watching her that he turned away, staring at the lights of the sub instead. When he heard a whooshing noise behind him, hope reared its head. She'd figured it out.

Spinning back to look, he realized the whooshing noise hadn't come from the flute.

Kim had unbuckled her helmet. It was still loosely attached to her head, water trickling in through the gaskets as she let the pressure equalize.

Horrified, he swam toward her, reaching for the helmet buckles, then pulling his hands back as he realized touching them might send water into her helmet so fast that it crushed her head.

"Don't give up!" He mouthed the words through his helmet, hoping she could hear him or read his lips. They had come too far to give up now.

Kim tightened her grip on the flute, bringing it up toward her helmet. She hadn't given up and was going to try to play it.

She wouldn't have much time. Not in water this cold. Not with a single lungful of air.

As water flooded over Kim's mouth and then nose, Flint shuddered.

There was one thing he could still do. When the helmet was full of water, he reached over and, as gently as he could, lifted it off her head.

Pain flashed across the young woman's face as she lifted the flute to her mouth and pressed her fingers on several holes. The pattern of holes in the flute was entrancing. As Flint stared, however, he felt something was wrong. A part of the pattern was missing. There! Just above Kim's thumb was a hole an alien hand could have closed. Flint extended his shaking hand and covered the hole with the tip of his finger.

Kim blew.

It was like hearing an ancient sea beast, something out of time, awakening from slumber. The sound waves rippled through the water. A note of homecoming. It was right. He knew it.

Sorrow overcame excitement as Flint looked at Kim and saw her panicked eyes and convulsing body. He was helpless to intervene as her convulsions softened into light twitches. Then, moments later, she stopped moving. Her brown eyes were open and unseeing in the water, ice crystals forming around her mouth.

She was dead.

And the door to the dome was opening.

Gently, Flint pried the flute from her frozen mouth, gripping it with all his strength.

A pattern had appeared in the circular door as the sound from the flute rippled across the cilia. Where the door had once been flat, it was now etched with organic, concentric circles. And at the center, a dark hole. It was the size of a pinprick at first and then grew in diameter, opening like the aperture on a camera until it was just large enough to fit an over-the-hill geologist.

Flint pulled himself through.

CHAPTER 31

Eva was surprised to find herself alive. Or at least, she assumed she was alive, because the world continued to exist around her.

She remembered her life before. The grind of graduate school, her relationship with Wulf, her downfall after he stole her research.

She remembered meeting Steve and thinking she was in love with him, because he was everything Wulf wasn't. Unambitious, perpetually relaxed.

She remembered giving birth to Sophie, the bright pain and triumph.

She was Eva.

But she was also someone else. When the threads pulled away from her eyes, the world was distorted, like she was looking at it underwater.

Could she move her limbs?

She could.

Feeling around herself, her hands brushed against a flexible, clear material. She was submerged in some kind of transparent, gel-filled tube. She still wasn't breathing, and the thought made her feel such panic that she directed her attention away from her lungs back to her vision. But all she could see was the gel and the tube encircling her. The shapes beyond were vague, green-gray geometry.

She was Eva, but she was also someone else. Another set of memories floated up, so inhuman the part of her that was Eva recoiled.

There was a distant star in a bright lenticular galaxy. There was life and advanced civilization. Strange festivals. Enormous hive-like structures covered the globe. Her people had big brains and long, slender limbs. They shared emotions with one another through complex, pheromonic antenna.

But their planet was dying, hollowed out by mining, the batteries and power cells that lined the megacities dimming year by year. They were not equipped for space travel. Their species was huge and interconnected. No space vessel could sustain a colony. But she had not wanted to die. None of them had. So, a group of technologists, the best biologists, and physicists in the system, had used their incredible understanding of biology and mutation to design a kind of radiation that could mutate an advanced carbon-based network into a biochemical signal that would replicate a memory.

She was alive. Their project had succeeded. She tried to straighten her antenna and flash them red and gold in joy, but something was wrong with her body. Her antenna were gone, severed. She would have to try and regrow them if she could, but everything was so *wrong*.

No. Not wrong. Different. Small, heavy, disconnected. She couldn't feel the hive. Fleshy sacs inside her struggled to operate in the gel matrix.

It wasn't just her body that was alien. She found she was also sharing her mind. With someone named Eva. She felt a hole in her head curl into the shape of the word, a newborn in her new home.

Eva.

She was Eva too. Her team had anticipated this, she reminded herself. Remolding chemical pathways was, at best, an imprecise art.

But she was alive.

THE SPACE FLINT SWAM into wasn't much larger than the crow's nest on the research station. As the hole closed behind him, casting him once again into darkness, Flint nearly screamed, his limbs thrashing against the impending entombment. As his arms and fins glided back and forth, however, the surrounding water lit up in splashes of glittering green. The bay was full of bioluminescent algae, and they glowed brighter the more he moved. Flint, calmed by the light, started to paddle his hands in the water, watching the pinpricks of green dance around his rubberized gloves.

Then, he felt himself pulled downward, and his feet tapped against a surface below him.

It was some kind of grate, a solid honeycomb of the same dark material the dome was constructed from. The water around him drained down through its irregular, organic holes.

In moments, the water was gone, and Flint found himself standing again on solid ground. With the water gone, he noticed another round dark circle on the far end of the room, like the one he had just come through. Another door.

He was in an airlock. As he reached to unclip his helmet, he hesitated. His gut told him to do it, that everything would be fine, that it was time to submerge himself in his new surroundings. Still, the last ember of self-preservation that hadn't been quenched by the terrible swim to the dome emitted a faint warning. *You don't even know if it's breathable air.*

Standing there with his helmet removed, he found himself holding his breath. Then he allowed his lungs to fill, reasoning that staying in the suit too long would poison him with nitrogen.

As far as he could tell, the air was just air. He breathed a sigh of relief and, peripheral vision restored, inspected his new surroundings.

The airlock had four gray walls and a drain, but as the door on the far wall spiraled open, Flint saw light. Crisp air, cool but not cold, ruffled his eyebrows. *Air circulation.*

He doffed his diving suit, feeling the excitement and alarm of a small child entering a large forest. Placing it on the ground, he rolled the flute into the waistband of his fleece under-suit.

Was this how Shackleton felt?

He was on a walkway, maybe ten feet wide. Walking toward it, alert to the lack of a railing, he saw...was it a city or a hive?

He thought it might be both. The space inside the dome was enormous. The gray material of the outer dome gave way to what looked like regular concrete.

Flint saw chunks of embedded granite and quartz that matched the surrounding environment. He guessed whoever had hollowed out the dome had used the rock to build the rest of the city. *Smart.*

The structures below him were constructed from barn-sized hexagonal blocks, stacked high in the center, maybe as high as three-quarters of the way up the dome. The outer rings were lower and irregular.

And the light. Lines of glowing blue and green and pink lit the edges of the hexagons like neon. None of them were bright on their own, but together they lit the dome into disco psychedelia.

What was the light source? Noticing a blue glow at his feet, Flint realized the walkway he was standing on was edged by a glowing blue strip. Bending down, he gasped as he saw the light coming from luminescent plant life bursting through the thin mesh.

It was beautiful, and Flint wanted to cry out to someone and show them what he had found. He wanted to radio the station's marine botanist and put her to work collecting samples. But there was no way to call anyone. A vision of ice crystals forming at the corner of dead brown eyes flashed across his vision.

He stood up and looked for a way down. Here and there along the high ridge were sections of wall he thought were meant as ramps. Their slopes were slightly less vertical, and they were covered in angular protrusions. They looked a little like the climbing walls on the cruise ships that sometimes passed through Antarctica. *Handholds.* He remembered Kim's robotic, alien hand, imagining it grasping these protrusions. *You have to stop thinking like a human.*

Every so often along the wall, where a human landscape designer might have installed a bench, there were shallow starburst depressions inlaid into the concrete. Flint wondered if these were meant to have the same functions as a bench and, if so, what the organisms that reclined in them might look like.

He walked for a few minutes along the walkway, stretching his legs, his fingers tucked into his armpits for warmth. His left hand, submerged for so long in icy water, was in bad shape, and he hoped to find something other than one of the climbing walls that would take him down into the city. No such luck.

Taking a deep breath, Flint turned toward the wall and lowered his foot onto one of the holds, grabbing a high protrusion with his better right hand. Lucky for him, the rubberized socks he'd worn under the diving suit worked about as well as climbing shoes, and he found the footholds stable.

He grabbed another hold with his left hand, and a stab of arthritic pain shot through his body with such force he nearly fell off the wall. He allowed himself to feel the pain, hoping the corresponding surge in adrenaline would help him make his way down. He moved his feet down again, then his right hand. He forced his left arm toward the next available hold, but his body rejected the movement.

It's just pain. You can survive the pain. You can't survive a hundred-foot fall.

He forced his fingers to grab the concrete. This time he let himself scream, in too much agony to fear what might hear him.

He continued this way for another sixty feet or so, favoring his right hand as much as possible. Twenty feet off the bottom, he reached a point where he had to use another hold with his left hand. His fingers had curled into claws, but he forced himself to extend them, aligning the tips with the top of the protrusion. He gripped. And his hand gave way. He tipped toward the empty air at his back as his feet slipped off their holds. Grasping at the wall, he grabbed the rough concrete with his right hand for long enough to avoid falling head-first. He tried to lean against the wall, feeling the concrete holds punch into his body as he slid down it, gaining speed.

As he hit the ground, he tried to roll but mistimed it. His ankle twisted under his weight, and a pop from his knee echoed across the smooth concrete surfaces around him.

He lay on the ground, feeling a fleeting regret the fall hadn't killed him. He was in more pain now, a constant dark shadow on his back. And he was hungry. As he realized it, he felt ridiculous. Injured and alone in an alien city, he was ready for lunch.

He stared up at the ceiling of the dome. Lines of light from the city below danced across its surface.

"Are you hurt?"

The voice came from his left. Flint spun his head, disoriented, but relaxed, when he saw a human face, rugged, with a matted blonde beard half gone to gray. The beard almost, but not quite, concealed a set of thin antenna emerging from the man's thin, flexible stalk of a neck, which itself was connected to a spindly, mantis-like body. As Flint sat up, he realized the person must be at least ten feet tall. *The monster in the hold.* Flint coughed.

"I twisted my ankle."

First contact with an alien life-form, and that was the best he could do. *Next time I'll hire a NASA speechwriter.*

"I'm Flint Hill. Doctor Flint Hill." *Sure. That'll impress him.* "I'm the research director at a station on the ice. Who are you?"

Flint focused on the human face. It reminded him of Bill.

"Bugsy Maroney. I was the cook on the *Bethany Rose.*"

"You can't be," Flint said. "You'd be over 200 years old."

The face raised an eyebrow at him as if he was a dim-witted child. Bill looked at new graduate students like that.

"I'm a few fathoms along, but I ain't dead. Things have changed for me somewhat down here."

"We found your ship," Flint said.

Suddenly, Maroney looked interested as Flint continued. "When you disappeared, your captain thought you were dead. But I guess you found this dome instead."

"Didn't *find* this dome. I built it," Maroney said, sounding offended. "From the ground up, with my own two..." he looked down at the location where hands would appear on a human body, seeming upset. He looked back at Flint and they stared at each other.

"Have you got any food?" Flint asked.

Flint was able to walk, though not without pain, and he followed Maroney as the tall, alien sailor wove through the honeycomb buildings on the outskirts of the city. Flint tried not to look at Maroney's body as they moved. The inhuman movement sickened him, and he didn't have anything in his stomach to spare.

"How come you got no pod?" Maroney said.

Flint frowned.

"What do you mean?"

"Your friends got pulled into the dome and stuffed in pods. How come you ain't with them?"

Eva. Flint felt a rush of excitement. Maybe she was alive.

"Can you take me to the pods?"

Maroney's head spun around on its stalk, and Flint's stomach lurched.

"Dinner first," the sailor said and shut his mouth tight.

CHAPTER 32

Eva floated in the thick gel, her thoughts moving as slowly as the viscous currents around her. There was little to do or look at, so she dozed in and out of sleep.

She was glad to be alive.

The first interruption to this haze was a metallic whirr, followed by a sucking noise and the movement of gel. Her awareness of her surroundings increased as the gel in the tube drained, floating her down to a grated floor. As her head emerged into the cool air, she coughed. Clear gel flowed out of her mouth, and she struggled for a moment to readjust to the sensation of breathing.

When the tube was drained, a wet click rang out from underneath her, and Eva found she was able to detach the flexible tubing material from a metallic ring near her feet. Pulling it over her head, she took a moment to find her footing before stepping out into the flatly lit room beyond.

It was a laboratory. Even without her new memories, Eva thought she would have understood that. She recognized lab benches and glassware. The proportions were off, however. Or at least, off relative to her human body. At this thought, she looked down at her body. *I've been breathing soup. Am I even human?*

She wasn't herself. Although she saw no changes to her physical form. She was clad in some kind of jumpsuit made from a silvery fabric.

A hypnotic movement caught Eva's eye, and she turned to see liquid swirling in a row of tubes identical to the one she had just emerged from. Light through the gel cast eerie, deep-sea waves on the floor.

Most of the tubes were empty, but two held the shapes of human beings. Eva felt a surge of excitement. Her people were there. Her family. A tidal wave of loss washed over her as she thought about her dying planet. Now they were so few, buds cut off the vine on a barren shore. The tubes were more than precious. They were essential.

Eva took slow, deferential steps as she walked over to the tubes. They ran from the laboratory floor to the ceiling, four feet in diameter, filled with gel. Only two were occupied.

Adams and Wulf. The rush of revulsion Eva felt whenever she thought about Wulf returned. Even through the gel, he looked like an asshole. A very sticky asshole.

Nausea rose up in Eva's gut as her revulsion for Wulf crashed against the tenderness she felt for the tubes, for the growing life within them. Her stomach twisted and she turned to the nearest corner to retch. Clear fluid, barely acidic, poured out of her body. The part of her that was Eva felt embattled, her emotions being reshaped to an alien purpose.

She couldn't look at the tubes again, not without bringing her internal conflict to a head. And she felt too weak for that, still.

Instead, she searched for a door, anywhere that would take her somewhere else.

Trying not to look at the viscous pool of her stomach contents, she stumbled across the room and through a tall slit in the wall, a three-foot gap that ran vertically from floor to ceiling.

She would be fine. She reassured herself as she moved down a smooth-walled corridor. She would be fine as long as she set up the beacon.

The beacon? What beacon? Eva stopped dead in the corridor, alarmed by the certainty with which the thought had come to her. She had a plan, she knew that. But the plan wasn't hers. It belonged to the *other,* a second set of memories and impulses riding her like a jockey. Could she resist it? Should she resist it?

If she did, her people would die.

There it was again.

Eva took a deep breath and shuddered as the cold air hit her weakened lungs.

I'll go to the beacon. And then I'll decide.

She stood upright, and as she did, she felt her spine stretch, extending upward toward the top of the corridor. She grunted. There was so much gravity here. More than there should be. It was intolerable.

It didn't matter. She could still activate the beacon.

Her muscles strained as her feet led her toward the center of the dome.

THE WAY MARONEY ATE was so astonishing Flint barely had time to be alarmed by the glowing pile of moss the sailor dropped on the floor in front of him. After depositing the glowing, tumbleweed-sized mass, Maroney skittered over to his own dinner, an enormous insect guarding his stash with his body. The skin of his neck started to ripple and twitch, like storm-tossed water, as if something within was seeking an escape. A flexible, fleshy proboscis emerged from Maroney's human throat releasing a chorus of pulpy squelches and moist gurgles, so organic and abhorrent it made Flint's stomach turn. Thick slow drips, like chilled honey, echoed as they hit the floor.

The proboscis excreted chartreuse liquid onto the moss pile, and a faint acrid odor invaded Flint's nose. He sneezed in response.

"G'bless you," Maroney said, his voice garbled as the tube blocked his tongue. A distant expression crossed his face, a mix between confusion and alarm. He didn't look like he remembered much about God. The tube shot back into Maroney's throat, and he covered his mouth in embarrassment.

"It's been long time, no people, table manners," he explained, looking away. Now Flint looked down at the moss. As he did, his stomach grumbled. He reached a hand toward the pile. As his fingers brushed the thin wisps, the moss lit up, the bioluminescence firing in a quick burst. The smell of the first piece he pinched off was earthy. Like a forest in the rain.

"Is this going to poison me?" he asked Maroney.

Maroney shrugged. "I eat it."

He'd never find Eva if his low blood sugar took him out. Hell, even if he had a Cornish pasty and a Guinness in front of him, she still might elude him. He chewed and swallowed, wincing as grit scraped his enamel.

He should have waited a minute to see if he broke out in hives or grew a second tongue, but his lizard brain was screaming at him to eat and so he pinched off more moss and chewed.

"Doctor Milroy's always trying to get me to eat more salad," he said.

Maroney's proboscis inched back out, and he ignored Flint, slurping his dis-solving moss instead. Flint doubted there was salad in either 18th-century England or outer space.

"Where do you get this stuff?" Flint asked.

Maroney shrugged. "I pick it."

"Do you grow it?"

"It grows, and I pick it."

For a two-hundred-year-old half-alien mariner, Maroney was incurious about his circumstances.

When Flint had eaten as much moss as he could bring himself to swallow, he cleared his throat and got on with it.

"Do you know how to find the other people in the dome?"

Maroney made a noncommittal noise.

"I'm looking for a woman," he said, half-expecting the sailor to return a lewd retort.

"Found you 'cause you screamed," Maroney said. "Only scream I heard."

"What do you do all day?" Flint asked, out of raw curiosity.

"No day or night in the dome. I build. Pick moss. Eat moss."

"Why did you flee your ship?" *I doubt 18th-century sailors were very tolerant of human-arachnid hybrids.* If only Maroney could have met Darwin. Still, Flint wondered.

"Had to build the dome," Maroney said. Flint sighed. It was like talking to a robot that was only programmed to respond to three questions.

"Are there others? Like you?" Flint asked.

Maroney stretched his limbs. Flint heard the soft rustling noise of chitin on chitin.

"You're here," Maroney said, as if Flint was stupid. "Time to build. You pick moss."

"I'm sorry, but I have to find my friend."

Maroney moved so suddenly Flint had no time to steel himself for the blow. In the space between one breath and the next, the sailor's chitinous arm shot out and knocked Flint onto the ground. He coughed and gasped and found he was pinned down, Maroney's mutated hand around his throat. The extended fingers made Flint feel ill.

He certainly has better reach than me.

Maroney's face, eerily distant, squinted at him.

"I build. You pick moss."

The hand around Flint's neck released, and he curled up, gasping.

"I think my foot is broken," he said. Surely, he was too old and arthritic for manual farm labor.

As Maroney stared at him, a transparent eyelid slid down across his sclera, moistening his eyes.

"If it's broke, it goes in the slime," Maroney said, with the assurance of a schoolboy reciting the pledge of allegiance.

Maroney moved out of the room so quickly Flint thought he heard the whoosh of air filling a vacuum. A moment later, the sailor returned with a plastic bucket filled with a gelatinous substance the color of moldy tofu.

The substance shivered as Maroney plonked it on the ground in front of Flint.

"Fix the foot," the sailor said, pointing at the bucket. As Flint stared inside, he realized the gel had the same photoluminescence as the moss. He gathered he was meant to plunge his broken foot into the stuff. If he didn't, he suspected Maroney would do it for him.

Wincing, he leaned over and began to remove the rubberized sock covering his swollen skin.

CHAPTER 33

The *OTHER* guided Eva to the center of the dome. It must have. The interlocking hexagonal structures around her all looked the same, constructed from the same mottled concrete. Still, her gut screamed that she was nearing the center of the labyrinth. The sense of progress was mostly internal, but after a little while, she noticed the lines of glowing mosses along the floors and walls of the corridor were changing in color from deep blue to ecstatic gold. The floor sloped steadily upward, and soon the endless identical corridors spit her out into a large, open space. Air flowed across her skin and she shivered, mesmerized by the enormous curve of the dome overhead.

In front of her, across an expanse of the same mottled concrete, was a tower. It had to be at least the height of a twenty-story building.

That's where the beacon is.

She looked for a door as she approached, but all she could see were circular windows that fed into the building. Each one was six feet off the ground. No glass or other obstacles blocked their openings, but she'd never get in without a ladder.

Reaching up, Eva felt along the lower edge of the nearest window, but the concrete there was smooth. Even with a firm handhold, she doubted she had the upper body strength to haul herself up. Again, oppressive gravity dragged her down into the earth. Eva took another breath, wishing she could get a little higher. As she stared at the opening, she imagined herself stretching upward.

The edge of the window got closer. Eva blinked, wondering if she had activated some kind of extending platform beneath her feet. She was almost tall enough to see inside the window. Maybe she could grab something now.

As she extended her arm to feel for a handhold, she almost vomited. She hadn't been raised up by some platform.

She had gotten taller. She had extended.

Inspecting her arm in front of her face, she saw it had lengthened. Had the gel in the tube added mass to her body? Or had she been stretched out, a human Gumby? Was this why she suddenly hated gravity?

She willed away any desire to get taller, hoping to stave off any more physical transformations, and reached back inside the window. *There!* She caught a ridge, her fingers squishing against threads of moss. Reaching her other hand in, she grasped and pulled, pushing off the ground with her legs.

Her chest scraped against the concrete floor with a thud as she pulled herself into the first room of the tower.

Scrambling to her feet, awkward in her new, stretched-out body, Eva was disappointed as she inspected her unfamiliar surroundings. It was another hallway, like the ones she had passed through on her way here. The floor was lit with troughs of glowing gold moss running near the walls. Still, she was getting closer. There were no turns to contend with now, just a long hallway running inward at a slight angle.

The end of the hallway contained something new. Another door, like the one that had blocked the entrance to the dome. She wished she still had the flute. Or even the replica flute. This door was smaller than the one leading into the dome, and her newfound alien instincts insisted it was simpler. She just had to hit one note. A single, perfect note. The world's most boring karaoke.

Eva couldn't sing. On Sophie's last birthday, her daughter had covered her ears and begged for a reprieve when Eva had tried to join the chorus. After that, Eva limited her role to cake provider and left the singing to Steve.

Sophie. Eva tried to imagine folding her daughter in a hug with her new, spidery limbs. It would be like wrapping a felt doll in wire.

The part of Eva that was the ***other*** protested this thought. ***We don't hug. She won't either after you activate the beacon.***

The cool detachment was so shocking Eva took a step away from the door. Then paused. But, of course, that was what she was here for. When she activated the beacon, the radiation that had produced her novel chemical memories would flow out across the Earth. Her people, so close to extinction, would live again. She was so lonely. Without her people, she was a head without limbs. None of her family and none of her drones.

The door would admit her. It had been designed to admit her. She just had to remember the note. An image crossed through Eva's brain of the end of a respiration cycle in the hive, the chirping and whirring calls that echoed in the air as the memory sharing ended, and the work cycle began. It was a song of commencement, calling the drones to work, igniting the creative energies of the hive heads. It was a golden sound, thrilled to celebrate new tunnels and hatching eggs. Igniting the beacon was nothing if not a beginning. She sang the note now, then cringed as a rattling screech hit her ears. It was wrong. All wrong. Her throat was malformed, squishy. How could joyful noise echo through this spongy meat?

She could do it, knew she could, and willed her throat to lengthen. While the gel could not return her old body, not entirely, it could help her return to her old work. The part of Eva that was still Eva tried to resist the mutation, but it was too late. The *other* had taken hold.

Eva sang again, and this time, she felt triumph. Her mutated throat produced a note that rang out through the air of the lab, a joyous vibration that washed across the doorway. The cilia there vibrated, and a small aperture appeared, widening to admit her.

The room beyond was more like the laboratory where Eva had woken up than the hallways she had just traveled through. It was hexagonal, maybe thirty feet across, lined with tall tables and buckets of gel. In the center of the room was a ten-foot-tall dodecahedron. Eva stared up at it, curious. Each face of the dodecahedron was some type of screen. Most were dark, but in a few places, the screens flashed with glowing patterns that were simultaneously alien and familiar.

She was seeing emotions, she realized. The emotions of the isolated people in this huge, empty hive. It was almost pathetic.

Two of the screens flickered with steady waves of amber. *Waiting. Maybe sleeping.* One flashed with gray interlocking circles, orderly and purposeful. *Work well done.* Near the bottom, almost out of her view, was a blazing yellow star banded with gray. *Struggle, but also hope.* Moving around and crouching to look at it more closely, a revelation washed over her.

"It's me. I'm the star," she said. Next to the yellow-and-gray screen was another, this one dimmer. Her lips curled into a frown as she looked at the red lines. *Pain. Injury.*

As she moved to stand up, Eva noticed for the first time there was a small moat running around the edge of the dodecahedron, about the size and depth of a Bundt cake pan. The moat was full of the same clear gel that had filled her tube. Resisting an alien urge to plunge her face into the gel, she settled instead for immersing her hands. The viscous substance surrounded her fingers and filled in the space under her nail beds.

This was one of her people's communication tools. She understood it now. It was like a telephone line. But instead of sound, the gel conveyed chemical signals and pheromones.

Yes, but who's on the other end of the line? Her left hand joined the right in the gel and she allowed her consciousness to flow outward, pulsing through the dome. A powerful feeling of emptiness ricocheted back to her. She should be feeling the emotions of the others in the hive, their needs, and their pride. Instead, she was trapped in a lifeless hive. ***Abandoned?*** The human part of Eva protested. It wasn't abandoned. There was no waste processing. She had assessed no cemeteries. The dome wasn't dead. It was waiting. A new development is about to go on the market.

It wouldn't be empty when she activated the beacon. Not if her research team had done their jobs.

A sensation from a distant corner of the dome caught her attention. Red lines of pain matched what she'd seen on the screen. Curious, she wiggled her fingers and sent her awareness toward it. A shock of pain rebounded toward her, but not before recognition struck.

Flint. Two things were clear to her. One, he was injured or had been recently. And two, he had the flute. It was there against his skin, and Eva felt a longing. How could she have let it go? How had it taken her so long to understand? The flute wasn't like the city. It was not a facsimile churned up from whatever materials the drones could pull from the ground. The flute had traveled through the stars, billions of years old, made to last. The research team on her dying planet had reasoned any species sufficiently advanced to implant chemical memories would have some understanding of sound and music. How could they not?

Eva felt her humanity resurface. Red anger washed across her eyes. These aliens were not benevolent. They had planned to hijack the nearest sentient species, rebooting their society in new bodies on a new planet. The flute was like an evil version of Carl Sagan's golden record. A message sent through space not to connect but to dominate.

Now, Eva ripped her hands out of the gel and pushed with her fragmented consciousness against the ***other***.

"You'll destroy us," she whispered.

The ***other*** scoffed. ***You eat animals for food. Intelligent, conscious animals. Pigs have emotions.***

Eva frowned as a bright ball of pain blossomed between her eyebrows.

Well, then try taking over a pig .

The pain disappeared, replaced by a thoughtful silence. Eva sighed.

"I have to find Flint," she said, forcing resolve into her voice.

I have to get that flute.

CHAPTER 34

FLINT STRETCHED HIS ANKLE as he looked down over the edge of a concrete bank into a wide crater filled with glowing moss. No pain, but the limb felt odd, like stiff new jeans.

He looked over at Maroney, who had led him here to what looked like an agricultural basin.

"How do we get down there?" he asked.

It was a twenty-foot drop. Maroney grunted and, before Flint could react, grabbed him around the waist. Hanging over the edge of the crater, Maroney passed Flint from his arms to his surprisingly prehensile legs, then dropped him the remaining six feet onto a soft pile of vegetation. Flint grunted in surprise rather than pain and watched as Maroney leaped gracefully to the ground beside him. With one long arm, the alien sailor directed Flint's attention to a cylindrical well about thirty feet away.

"You pick moss for the well. I'm going to build."

"Wait!" Flint said. "Tell me what's going on."

Maroney looked incredulous.

"Moss. Moss for the well."

He gestured once again toward the structure.

"What is the moss for?"

"Food. Slime. Light." Maroney repeated these things with slow disinterest.

"I'd like to take a look around," Flint said. "Where are the stairs?"

"You pick moss. I build."

With that, Maroney skittered up the nearly vertical adjacent wall with a smooth spring and disappeared beyond Flint's sight.

Flint took what felt like a long time to explore his surroundings, walking the circumference of the crater until he started to see his own footprints in the moss again. As far as he could tell, there was no way out. He didn't think it was supposed to be a prison. Maroney certainly hadn't struggled to leave.

Maybe it's a nursery. Or a pasture.

He shivered at this last thought.

There was little to look at. Everything in the crater except for the well in the center was covered in a lumpy, three-foot-high sponge of bioluminescent turquoise moss.

The well turned out to be a chute. It angled away from the pasture at a steep grade, headed toward the center of the dome. Flint wondered where it let out. He imagined whirring blades. Or maybe an incinerator.

He debated climbing down to check, but realistically, he'd never be able to climb back up. For a while, he lay on the ground near the well, staring at the ceiling of the dome and trying to nap. The unchanging light disoriented him. At the research station, even in the dead of summer or winter, there were small changes throughout the day in the quality of light. Here there was only an endless glow.

Flint's efforts to nap were futile, and eventually, he was bored enough to start working, picking huge handfuls of moss and tossing them down the well in clumps, listening for any sound that would tell him what was on the other end of the tunnel. But there was nothing—the vegetation disappeared into the chute soundlessly, slipping against the smooth sides of the chute. When his hunger returned, he ate a handful of the moss. It tasted just like the stuff Maroney had given him. *I hope the grit is where all the nutrients are.*

It was food, but it could also be turned into a gel that could knit bones back together. Flint wondered if this moss species had come from somewhere on Earth or if it had come from...whatever had transformed Maroney. Collapsing back on the ground, he felt at his waistband for the hard cylinder of the flute. Unrolling the waistband, he inspected the pattern of holes.

"You haven't lost it!" The loud voice shocked him, and he looked around at the moss until he realized the voice was coming from above him, along the rim of the crater. He glanced up and found Eva's face staring back at him.

"You're alive!"

"In more ways than one," she said and leaned over the edge. He walked toward her, closing the distance between them until he was near enough to really see her.

He swallowed. Watching Maroney move through the dome had been enough. But seeing the mutations on someone he knew, someone he liked, was a different story.

Noticing the shock on his face, Eva stared down at her limbs. Two flickers of disgust washed across her face. The expressions were similar but distinct. They conveyed the impression of someone not at home in their body.

"We are altered," she agreed.

We? Flint strained to see behind her. Was Adams with her?

Whatever Maroney was, Eva was on her way there. She wouldn't meet his eyes. After a moment, he realized why. She was staring at the flute. He stepped back.

"What happened? Your sub flooded. I thought you might be dead, but Maroney said you were in a tube."

Now she looked at him. She shook her head and coughed. "I don't remember everything that happened at the end, but Adams was in cahoots with Wulf."

She told him about the trip in the sub, about the threads piercing the hull. When she described waking up in the gel, Flint grew wary. *She's leaving something out. Something about why she just used the royal "we."*

He told her about following the sub in the diving suits, about the long swim through the dark tunnels.

"Kim's dead," he said in a low voice.

"It's okay," Eva said. "You did what really mattered. You brought us the flute."

Now, she extended a long-fingered hand over the edge of the crater. If Flint stood on his toes, he'd just be able to reach her.

Instead, he took another step back. Eva smiled, but not before he saw anger flash across her face.

"Who did you mean when you said *we*?" he asked.

"Wulf and Adams are still in their tubes," she said, deflecting. As Flint took another step back, Eva traversed over the lip of the crater and onto the moss. When she rose back up to her full height, Flint could see she was over six feet tall. It suited her. She looked elegant and agile, clad in some kind of silvery fabric. Ignoring this last thought, he skittered back toward the well as she drew closer, a predatory smile on her face.

"I'm the antiquities expert. I should hold it."

Feeling desperate as she loped toward him, Flint held the flute out over the lip of the well.

"If you come any closer, I'll drop it," he said.

"No!" When Eva screamed, she sounded only half human. Something about the way sound vibrated through her throat had changed. It was horrifying, yet familiar. *She sounds like the flute.*

"Please," Eva said. "We'll explain everything. But we need it. You're killing me. You're killing a planet."

Flint's hand shook, and he felt compelled to return to Eva's side. To give her the flute. His newly mended right foot moved of its own volition in her direction. Flint started to pull the flute back toward his body when suddenly, his hand cramped.

That old, familiar pain roared back to full strength like a bonfire, traveling up to his elbow. His fingertips were numb, and before he could resist, he felt his hand unclench. The flute plinked down onto the smooth surface of the chute and slid into the darkness beyond. He stared at the empty space where it had been until something flashed in his peripheral vision.

He turned his head just in time to see Eva, sprinting on all fours, dive into the chute after the flute. Banging against the curved lower surface, she began to slide, accelerating on the frictionless chute. Flint tried to grab her but only succeeded in banging his useless hands on the rim of the well.

"Eva!" he shouted. An alien whoop echoed out from the hole and faded into silence.

Sweat beaded on Flint's face as he considered the possibilities. If the chute fed into an incinerator or a whirring titanium blade, it would be taken care of. So would Eva, for that matter. But if the flute and Eva were still around...

He couldn't let whatever was wearing Eva's body have the flute. He knew that just as he knew the impulse driving him toward the dome had not been a noble sense of mission but a lure.

He sat on the edge of the well, pulled his legs over, took a deep breath, and let himself fall.

Flint picked up speed, and soon the darkness of the tube swallowed him. He had grown accustomed to the flat, persistent light inside the dome, and now he screamed in the dark, trying to swallow his fear and waiting to discover if he was about to be dropped into certain death or agonizing injury.

The angle of the chute never changed, but soon, he realized it was getting light again. Wherever it ended, he was about to reach it. He ran his arms around the edge of the tube, trying to slow himself, but found no purchase on the smooth gray surface. His scream returned, and the light grew bright. Then it blinded him, as he fell through the air and landed in a gel that covered his head and blocked his nostrils. Lips pressed shut, he struggled against the viscosity. The last time he'd tried to swim was on his disastrous honeymoon, and his arms flailed.

You just swam across half the Amundsen Sea. Calm down. He stilled himself for a moment, then kicked his feet, undulating like a spoon through Jello. His head surfaced, and he gasped for air, flipping on his back to see if he could float. Near the surface, great clumps of moss bobbed.

They're dissolving.

Was the gel some kind of slow-acting acid, turning him into the dome's equivalent of Soylent Green?

No. He had put his foot in the gel, and his foot hadn't dissolved. And Eva had been submerged in gel in her tube. She'd said she'd even breathed it. Flint took in another lungful of air to reassure himself he didn't have to go that far.

She didn't dissolve, but she didn't come out unscathed either...

Where was she? Flint swiveled his head in a wide circle. The pool of gel was maybe twenty feet across, and it was clear she wasn't in it.

Which meant there must be a way out. Staying on his back, he kicked his feet toward the edge of the pool and found the edge was barely a foot above the surface. Grabbing the lip with both hands, he pulled himself over and collapsed onto dry land.

Panting on the ground, gel sliding off his body, Flint noticed a small object lying discarded nearby. A knife. Flint picked it up. It looked old, and well cared for. Eva probably could have identified its age, but Flint suspected it was from the *Bethany Rose*.

I guess Maroney hasn't given up all the old ways.

As Flint tucked the knife into his waistband, he noticed a sloppy spot on the ground five feet from where he'd hauled himself out of the pool. Footprints led away from the gel to a circular aperture in a nearby wall.

Flint followed the trail and clambered through the circular window into the next hallway. This went only a short distance before it ended at a twisting staircase.

The climb was long, but Flint was reassured by the sight of occasional globs of gel on the concrete steps. He was still on the right track.

He felt certain he was in the heart of the dome now, and no doors or windows presented themselves until, finally, he emerged through a hole in the ceiling onto a wide, open balcony. As he suspected, he was at the center of the dome. The balcony was immense, the diameter of a football field. He was near the edge, and the view of the alien city beyond the balcony made him gasp. At this distance, the bioluminescent algae he'd encountered everywhere coalesced into intricate patterns. The breathtaking fractals made the city look like a neon Persian rug.

Another glob of goop lay on the ground, but it was hardly helpful. There was only one conceivable place on the balcony where Eva could have gone: a giant antenna in the center, stretching toward the top of the dome.

Eva stood facing away from him, staring at a tall instrument panel, the flute clutched in her hand. As Flint approached, she wrapped her lips around the flute and played a few weak notes. They vibrated through his bones, and his right foot lit up with a tingle. The notes died off, and Eva turned. There were tears in her eyes.

"It's not working. My hands are wrong," she said. Flint thought about Kim's mechanical alien hand, about how he had helped her hit the right notes under the water. He wouldn't help Eva now. Not after what he'd learned.

"If you don't help me, we'll all die," she said. Her voice was different now, underlain with whirrs and clicks.

"Tell me what you mean. Explain it to me clearly," Flint said, trying to buy time as much as anything. He watched her take an unsteady breath, looking for all the world like a woman at war with herself. She coughed and, a moment later, answered him.

"My planet was dying. So, my people built a device that could transfer our chemical memories to another species. We made hundreds of thousands of them and shot them into the universe. The devices emit a kind of..." she paused, sounding like an unprepared linguist asked to interpret a quantum physics lecture. "Radiation is the closest word. It's not quite right. When I activate the beacon, the memories will spread. My people will live again. The hive is prepared for them."

Flint's stomach sank.

"So whatever happened to you and Maroney will happen to everyone?"

"Is that the drone? I sensed there was a drone."

Flint thought about Maroney's moss, his relentless desire to collect and build.

"What do you mean by drone?"

Eva paused. "Our species is not like yours. You're independent. Our species is more collective and more distributed. The drone builds. The mind thinks."

Flint frowned. "That hardly seems fair to the drones. Sounds like second-class citizenship."

Eva shook her head, eyes wide and unblinking.

"Is your foot a second-class citizen of your body?"

Flint shrugged. "If I've been on my feet all day, it feels that way."

"I'm a brain without my feet and eyes," Eva said, "that's the best way I can describe it."

"What about Eva? Is she still in there?" Flint said.

She blinked. "I'm Eva. I am. I'm just...more."

The control panel beside her flashed with a complicated pattern of green and blue. Eva's head whipped around, and her eyes took in the image. She tapped a few buttons, and a familiar voice crackled through an indentation on the panel.

"This is Rear Admiral Vernon Ash for...the dome. I repeat. Rear Admiral Vernon Ash. Is anyone inside?"

Eva-not-Eva stared at the panel, tapping her chin with a long finger.

"If you don't respond, they might just nuke us. This place is sturdy, but it's not *that* sturdy." Flint felt ridiculous. What the hell was he doing? *Buying time.*

"If they pick up a weird signal spreading across the Earth from an alien dome, they're not going to waste their time wondering what it is. They're going to hit us with every ounce of firepower their submarines can haul here. They'll crack us open like a Kinder egg."

Thinking about the penguin colonies such a blast would obliterate, Flint felt angry. That much energy would melt a huge hole in the ice shelf. It would be like dousing an ice cube in kerosene and throwing it in a volcano. Humans had already done a number on the climate, but that would be the icing on the...well, ice. On the other hand, a nuclear weapon would do a bang-up job of preventing the planet from being turned into space aliens.

Eva pressed a button on the console.

"Rear Admiral Ash?" she said.

There was a sharp intake of breath on the other end of the line. Flint didn't think Ash had expected to reach anyone.

"Rear Admiral? This is...well, let's just say it's Eva Ward."

"Doctor Ward. Are you alright? Are you being held hostage?"

"That's a complicated question. Let's say I am speaking on behalf of the people who built this dome."

Flint heard the admiral take two long, slow breaths.

"Then let me extend the greetings of the United States government and, more broadly, the people of Earth. We do not seek war, but we will not shrink from it."

Eva snorted, sounding like herself. Flint had to agree. This speech was a little feeble for first contact.

"Is Adams with you?" the rear admiral said, proceeding cautiously. "Are you alone?"

"I'm certainly not alone," Eva said. "We'll be in touch."

She clicked the button again and the panel went dark.

Flint, feeling the weight of the knife against his leg, stepped forward.

"I'll help you play the flute," he said.

Eva stared at him, dubious.

"I helped Kim," he said. "How do you think we got inside?"

Eva looked from him to the flute, wary. He took another step. Reached out to her with his left hand. As he did, he slipped his right hand into his waistband.

"You don't know the notes," Eva said.

"I knew them outside. I could feel them. The flute wants to be played. Maroney used the gel to fix my foot. I'm changing too, Eva. Let me help."

When he said her name, a small jolt ran through her body. When she looked at him next, her eyes were more Eva than alien. It was the worst possible moment for a change, and Flint felt lousy with guilt as he stabbed the knife into the joint between Eva's thigh and hip. He had no idea what was happening to her bones, but he would bet money her femoral artery was still pumping blood to her legs.

She screamed and stumbled backward. Her eyes watered, and clear second eyelids slid across them, sweeping away the tears. She punched at Flint with a long, strong arm, but he dodged this first blow. As Eva spun around for round two, she slipped on a quarter-sized pool of blood that had run down her leg onto the floor, sending her crashing onto the concrete head first. There was a crack, and an opalescent fluid dripped down her nose onto the floor. As she reached up to touch it, Flint leaped on top of her, pinning her spidery limbs to the ground with the weight of his body. He raised the knife above his head, then hesitated as he saw Eva staring back at him.

"Do it," she whispered. "Tell Sophie I'm sorry."

Flint brought the knife down.

Before it made contact, a freight train hit him from behind.

"Bloody bastard!" a male voice cried.

Maroney. He had slammed Flint down on top of Eva, and now he pulled him off her, rolling him onto his back and delivering stabbing strikes to the chest with his thin limbs. Something inside Flint crunched, and he felt cold. He tried to raise his knife hand, but Maroney knocked it down and raised his right arm for a final strike.

If the blow hit him in the head, he would die. Flint was sure of it.

"You hurt the head!" Maroney shrieked. Flint felt blood soaking into his pants. Eva's, not his.

"If you don't put pressure on her wound, she'll die," Flint said.

Maroney hesitated, looked over, and as quickly as he'd struck Flint, he scurried over Eva's crumpled body and located the knife wound. Flint took a breath and scrambled to his feet as Maroney tried to make his alien hand the right shape to apply pressure.

"If you take your hand off that cut, she'll spill the rest of her precious blood all over your roof. You have to take her to the gel right now."

Maroney looked down at Eva. He hesitated no longer than the space of a blink, folding her smaller body into his arms and leaping at top speed to the staircase that had led Flint to the roof.

When the black receded from the edges of Flint's vision, he pulled up his shirt and found a purple circle the size of a grapefruit. He pressed it with a careful finger, and it was like a wet sponge. Fighting through the pain, he dragged himself over to the instrument panel and poked at the button he'd seen Eva press to communicate with Ash.

"Hello?" He rasped out the word and waited in silence. Miraculously, someone was listening.

"Rear Admiral Ash here. To whom am I speaking?"

The admiral was formal and remote.

"It's Flint. I'm alone. As far as I can tell."

"You sound injured."

"You should see the other guys. Well, girls. Well, Eva and her... alien brain buddy."

As the words juddered out of him, he realized he was in shock.

"Are you telling me you wounded Eva?"

"I know it sounds bad, but she was trying to fire off the big antenna."

There was a long pause as Ash conferred with someone on the other end of the line. Time was of the essence, and Flint didn't want to bury the lead.

"Here's the deal. They've got some kind of radiation-emitting device. If it goes off, it's gonna mutate Earth's population. Remember the guy we found in the *Bethany Rose*?"

"I do," Ash said, his voice clipped.

"We're all about to get a lot better at dunking basketballs," Flint said. He swallowed. "Right now, I'd bet cold money you're tempted to send the U.S. government's biggest fireworks down the lava tube after us and call it a day. But you better call up NOAA first."

"Why is that?"

"Because melting a big hole in Antarctica could cause catastrophic climate effects. Change the sea levels, and increase flooding. It'll screw with the weather and the fisheries. And I'm not talking about a few bad days. I'm talking about a bye-bye-no-more-dinosaurs extinction-level event."

"How do I know you're not working for the other side?" Ash asked.

"I don't know. I don't think I am," Flint said. "At least, not yet."

"Not yet?"

Flint stared down at his foot. "Look, Rear Admiral. We're not talking about alien hordes here. There's Eva and one of the sailors from the *Bethany Rose*. He built this place. Maroney. I don't think he can activate the beacon, though. She's the brains of the operation. Adams made it into the dome, too, along with some guy named Wulf. They might be dead or they might be skittering mutants now. These things are long-lived, but they're organic. They're just bugs. And I haven't seen a lot of gun towers around. Or flame throwers, or vats of burning alien acid.

We can hunt them down, I think. You just need someone to open the front door for you."

"I take it you're volunteering?" Ash said.

"Sort of. I don't really understand their technology. Not yet, anyway."

"As much as I'd love to send you to get a second PhD in xenotechnology, we're a little pressed for time."

"Well, I have an idea. It might help me think like the enemy," Flint said. "And to be honest, it might be the only way I can survive my injuries."

Black began to swirl in the edges of his vision, and Flint sank to the ground. It might work. *It has to work.*

CHAPTER 35

Soon, Flint was back in the basement, staring at the moss chutes and the big pool of gel. The topaz-colored goo wobbled. Its photoluminescence seemed brighter now, like glitter in gelatin. Maybe he was imagining things. He'd passed out once on his way down the stairs, waking up an indeterminate amount of time later with a goose egg on his head as a souvenir.

Now, the pool of goop glittered in welcome. Flint grabbed the lip with one arm. As he pulled, a rending pain shot through his chest, and he gasped. *Shit. I think I just punctured a lung.* His chest was beginning to feel heavy and wet.

Surely, he hadn't come all this way just to be stymied by a five-foot wall. He refused to be Moses, staring helplessly at the promised land. In a last-ditch effort, he reached over the lip of the pool and cupped the glowing gel between his hands. It felt cool on his palms, and he raised it to his lips. Taking a last breath of air, he buried his nose in the gel and breathed in.

The sensation was unpleasant. His brain screamed that he was putting the wrong thing in the wrong tube. The gel coated his trachea, then spread into his chest. He could feel it spreading inside of his lungs. He wanted to cough, to sputter but forced himself not to. He had to wait for the magic.

The gel seemed even more inviting now, warm and comforting. And it appeared to have had the analgesic effect he'd hoped for, dulling the pain that blossomed from whatever bone shard was stabbing him in the heart and lungs. Flint tried moving his arms again, and, the last of his human adrenaline screaming through his body, just barely managed to pull himself over the lip of the pool. He landed with a slick flop, his sigh of relief only moderately agonizing. The gel enveloped him, a warm insectoid womb that would consume him completely. He could let go now, let his mind sink into his brain stem, and let the aliens run the show for a while.

No. I have to hold on. I'm Flint Hill, and I can share my brain with an alien, but I'll be damned if I let it evict me.

He thought about all the things that made him himself. His years of experience as a geologist. The deep camaraderie with his research team. The pain in his hands, which had made him more crotchety at a much younger age than the people around him deserved. The ice. The beautiful white-blue expanse of ice, the prismatic twilights. The terrible winters.

There it was. Screw the humans. Flint would do it for the ice. He'd be damned if he let Ash blast a hole through his home.

As the gel filled his lungs, he wrapped his mind around an image filled with stark whites and blues.

Eva woke only in flashes now, momentary bursts in which her old self reclaimed her consciousness. In these sensory interludes, she barely had time to think.

I've been shuffled into the passenger's seat of my own body.

First, there was a deep blackness, filled with red undertones and pain. Some part of her understood she was only conscious of this because she was near death. Neither she nor her alien jockey had the energy for a contest of wills. There were fragmented memories, a mad dash through the honeycomb of buildings, and then she was back in the laboratory where she'd first awoken. She was being tended to, first by the drone who had rescued her from the roof after Flint had betrayed her.

He was only trying to stab one of us.

If she lost enough blood, she guessed it wouldn't matter which one.

Eva faded in and out, until she came to, and realized she was staring into Sigmund Wulf's face. It was distorted by the gel in the tube, but she was confident it was him. No one else could set off such immediate crimson rage. The anger kept her grounded in her own mind, and she used the wave of adrenaline to force her arms through the gel to the place where the tube attached to its housing. As she yanked it up, a tsunami of gel spilled across the concrete floor. Wulf skittered away from it, and Eva had to blink several times to understand what she was seeing.

His face was familiar, but his body was fully transformed. He was at least eight feet tall, now, his arms stretched and thinned to twice their normal length. The fingers on his arms had lengthened and moved, his index fingers twisted down and hooked so it resembled a second thumb. Lines of fleshy threads covered his throat, waving like seagrass.

Trying not to lose focus, Eva turned her attention back to Wulf's still-punchable face. The familiar rage returned, and she spewed gel from her lungs as she squared on him, ignoring the discomfort as cold air flowed into her lungs.

"You bastard," she said and pulled her arm back to punch him in the jaw.

A sensation stopped her dead in her tracks, and the glint of a reflection in a glossy metal panel on the opposite wall told her why. She had transformed at least as much as Wulf. She touched the fleshy tendrils of flesh at her throat with a cautious hand. They weren't sensitive to the touch, but as her fingers brushed across them, her brain flashed with new information. Anger. Confusion. Fear. It was like the information she'd gotten from the gel. She had acquired a sixth sense, breathing in her own emotions.

It must be pheromones. It's why they developed the gel.

Well, if the only thing left of Wulf was his face, then that's what she would punch. She balled her fingers into a fist, discovering her hand had grown a flexible, claw-like protrusion on her wrist, near the fleshy part of her thumb. Despite her fingers' alien appearance, her new hand looked familiar.

Kim's robot hand.

But Kim was dead. Frozen in the ocean.

It serves her right for stealing the flute!

The thought fought for space in Eva's brain, and only her anger at Wulf allowed her to resist it.

Eva realized she'd been standing with her balled fist in the air, aimed straight at her ex's face. There was no sense in wasting a good setup.

She let fly with a blow, shocked at the force with which it connected. Unsteady on his spindly limbs, Wulf tumbled back, tripping over an abandoned length of tubing on the floor. Eva dropped to all fours and ran toward him, balancing over him on tripod limbs as she hit him again. This time his lip split open. An un-Wulf-like expression of sorrow crossed his face.

"Why are you crying? You're the reason we're here!" Eva shouted. She grabbed his throat, pressing her fingers into the ridges of cilia there.

Now he screamed for real, force-fed a double helping of Eva's rage.

"Shut up!" she said.

There was a moment of silence. Disgusted, she let go of his throat. He coughed and then formed a single word.

"Eva."

The sound of her name on his lips made her even angrier. Why did he sound betrayed?

Because he's not Wulf.

The voice of the **other** filtered up through her consciousness until it floated at the surface of her thoughts. She wasn't alone, and neither was he.

There was more, though. A double familiarity. Wulf and...

She grabbed his hand and pressed it to her throat, drinking in his emotions. Anxiety, obsession...

...and *love.*

Eva snorted at the absurdity. But there it was. Wulf loved her. *No. Wulf doesn't love me. It's someone else. He's got his own alien jockey.*

Eva's new memories clicked as she recognized the person staring out of Wulf's eyes. They had created the mindset project together a million years ago. They had carved the flute from his mother's chitin.

The ***other*** rose up again, gently this time, and seized Eva's body for its own. Her crushing grip on Wulf's wrist relaxed into the caress of a friend. More than a friend, in fact. They hadn't just worked together, they had shared gel during the respiratory cycle, emotions flowing back and forth between them until they were practically the same person. Tears welled in Eva's eyes. A billion years had gone by, and they were finally together again. Wulf placed his hand on Eva's throat and golden joy flashed between them, flowing in a looping cycle. Their planet had died, but they had saved themselves.

Eva's anger surged, and she fought for control against her alien rider. She had once promised herself that she would jump off the Statue of Liberty before she would allow herself to get back together with Wulf. Billion-year-old alien romance be damned, she was going to keep her promise. It took her entire force of will to wrest control from the ***other*** and pull her hand away.

Eva considered fulfilling a lifelong dream and kneeing him in the balls, but as she stared at the cilia around his throat, she wondered if he had any.

Flint said the sailor he met was 200 years old. She wanted to vomit when she imagined spending centuries with Wulf, but there was nothing left in her body to expel.

She wanted to kill him, but the hate was something to hang onto. Still, she couldn't let him get the flute.

Because it's mine.

Brushing this alien thought away, she decided to punch Wulf once more, for the road.

As she drew her arm back, something hit her from the side. Her punch went wild and she stumbled, spinning to see Dr. Adams crouched low, holding his ground a few feet away. There was nothing human in his face. Adams had given up, allowing his new alien memories to consume him. Eva felt the tension as she looked at him. This man had been an authority, back on the dying planet. He'd almost been a king. Eva resisted the urge to wave her arms in the intricate dance, to show the head that the body obeyed. Focusing instead on her hatred of Wulf, she remembered what Adams had told her.

"You said humans didn't deserve this planet. But these aliens aren't any better. They killed their home and now they want to kill ours."

Adams's eyes barely registered the argument. Instead, he delivered an eye-watering blow to Eva's breastbone and dug his fingers into her throat. The emotions were so overwhelming Eva wanted to scream. Disapproval, and worse. He was threatening to isolate her from the hive. An image rose in her brain of a penal colony on her old planet, of people whose emotion-sensing organs had been burned off with chemicals. Too unfit for communal living, they were denied sustenance from the hive, loners sentenced to scavenge wild mosses in the out-lands.

Eva raised a fist to strike him, to punish him for threatening her with this cold darkness. But she found she could not bring her arm down. Her new anatomy would not obey. She tried two more times, arms hanging in the air until her eyes welled with frustrated tears. Instead, she turned and ran through the nearest gap in the wall, her body crunching and popping as it contorted to an unnatural shape to fit.

I know the city better than they do. I'll never let them find the flute.

CHAPTER 36

Despite his arthritis, Flint had never been obsessed with youth. Given a choice between fixing his hands and being nineteen again, he would have picked his hands every time.

The renewed sense of vigor he felt when he left the gel vat was more of an oddity than a pleasant surprise.

His suspicions had been correct. He probed his new memories carefully, with the curiosity of a good graduate student, trying to surf the waves of new information without sinking and being consumed. As gel drained off his body, he approached a nearby instrument panel, tentatively pressing a button. Accessing his new memories felt like programming a new VCR using a poorly translated manual. Difficult, but possible with a little trial and error. There was a hole in the panel, and Flint placed a tentative finger inside it, feeling gel envelop the tip. The gel, he understood, acted as a kind of social glue and emotional conduit. It was used in interfaces to predict user desires. Flint wanted to open comms with Rear Admiral Ash, and so the nearby display guided him to the set of commands that would allow him to achieve this. He didn't think there was much in the way of data security or firewalls in this system. The aliens had assumed anyone who understood it well enough to hack it would need to use it with as few restrictions as possible.

"Rear Admiral Ash speaking." The voice wasn't audible, and it took Flint a moment to realize he was "hearing" it through the gel. He felt a wave of panic as he hoped the communications could travel both ways and angry static, anxiety incarnate, blasted him through the gel. The static continued as he assembled his thoughts, and finally, he willed a message through the network.

"I have the intel about the building I need. How quickly can you get to the door I came in?"

"We're still on cleanup duty from the EMP, but I've got my people rigging the escape pods from one of our nuclear subs to a small motorized undersea sled. I'd say an hour. Maybe two."

"I've still got a hold of myself," Flint said. "But I don't know what I'll be in two hours. I'll try to hang on long enough to put down the drawbridge."

"Is that key tactical information, or are you being ironic again?"

"It was a metaphor. The door's a big circle into an airlock. Opens from the center. Straightforward."

"Copy that. Will you be able to communicate along the way?"

The control panel produced an answer. There were comms at the door, but they were short-range only. Not much better than a doorbell.

"Not until you're close. I mean, really close."

"Copy that. We'll make contact as soon as possible. Ash out."

All Flint had to do was go back to the door and let the Navy in without letting anyone get their hands on the flute. Flint stared at the flute nestled in a pile of moss. He'd decided not to bring it into the gel with him, where it could communicate with the city. Now, he ripped a strip of fabric off his under-suit and carefully wrapped the flute, trying not to make skin-to-skin contact as he rolled it back into his trousers. *If what I have can still be called skin, that is.* Then, picking his knife up from where he'd hidden it under a clump of moss, he prepared to make the trek.

EVA RAN THROUGH THE city. The gravity was heavy, but her limbs were strong and light, and she felt a certain amount of pride in the loping stride. As a human, she'd always been miserable at running. Now, she understood why Steve had run all those half-marathons. Her adrenaline was pumping and the steady tap-tap-tap of her feet on the concrete corridor was lulling. Looping around the buildings, she rested inside a hexagonal concrete room and surveyed her new knowledge of the city. She couldn't let Adams and Wulf find her. Adams might kill her, and she couldn't stand to look at Wulf. But they would have to look for her cell by cell, and Wulf was poorly equipped for tedium. She would be almost impossible to find.

Unless she accessed a terminal. Then, she'd leave a pheromonal thumbprint at her access point, a signal she was contributing to the hive. Of course, in that case, she'd be able to see their access points as well.

An access terminal presented itself a few rooms away, inside some kind of gel refining center. Soon, she would know where they were. She vowed to use the comms net at lightning speed.

When she plunged her hands into the gel, it gave her little information. Adams and Wulf had accessed the terminal in the pod lab several times, but that was all.

Wait. Eva concentrated, the gel enveloping her hands. Her brain itched, rubbed wrong by the unfamiliar chemical signals, which only part of her understood.

A call had gone out. *Out? Out where?* Her fingers tingled, and the approximate location assembled itself in her brain.

Flint.

He wasn't dead. He had the flute, and he knew what it was for. But who would he have called? It was unlikely he had sent a final missive to his loved ones. The old man was a bone-deep loner. Which left one option: He must have called Ash.

If the Navy wanted in, they only had a few options. Flint must have been headed to open the top of the dome.

He can't. They'll destroy the flute. They'll exterminate my people, once and for all.

Eva's mind twisted inward, her two selves coalescing behind a common goal. Half of her wanted to save him, and half of her wanted the flute.

She pulled her fingers out of the terminal and started running in a random direction. There was no reason to let Adams and Wulf track her down before she was ready.

Her brain was folding in on itself, possibilities doubling and redoubling. A bright pinprick of pain pierced her somewhere near the top of her head, the screech of an overworked feedback loop. Picking up the pace, Eva pumped her arms and her long legs, running faster than she ever had before, leaning into her turns as she cornered hallways and corridors, leaping through portholes until she was too exhausted to think about anything but the next step. Oxygen raced through her lungs and she ran, ran, ran until the pinprick of pain subsided.

Picking a random building, she collapsed into a heap inside, gasping for breath. The hard ground cooled her hot skin. When her breathing slowed, she pushed off the ground, looking above her for guidance. She fought the urge to fully embrace the alien inside and felt she was losing her will to keep going.

FLINT'S EVEN PACE ALONG the corridors gave him time to probe his recent memories and impulses. The part of him that was Flint wanted to be cautious, to maintain a wall against the alien invader. But it was useless. He wasn't living in a remodeled house. He *was* a remodeled house. Now, as he traveled through the sloping concrete corridors, in and out of hexagonal honeycombed rooms, he felt a sense of respect and pride.

Good build. The heads will be pleased.

What had Eva said? *Is your foot a second-class citizen of your body?* Bending down to pick and swallow an aquamarine tuft of moss from the corridor floor, Flint thought he understood. He wasn't a head, a thinking brain. He was a foot.

Maybe it's better. Maybe there's less will there to dominate me.

Some indeterminate amount of time later, he was forced to reassess that hypothesis. He came to with no knowledge of the past few minutes, finding himself at the bottom of a circular pasture like the one Maroney had left him in. There was an enormous ball of moss in his arms, and as his senses regained dominion over his body, he found himself throwing it into the circular well at the center of the pasture. The action gave him a sense of deep, lingering pleasure. He was nourishing the city, exactly where he was supposed to be.

The cylinder of the flute was hard against his hip bone, and Flint cleared his head with a hearty shake. *The door. I have to open the door.*

This pasture was identical to the one he'd been in earlier, and he stared at the concrete wall, feeling like an idiot for dropping himself down another well. He had walked straight into a trap he'd set himself.

Earlier, Maroney had gotten out of a similar pasture with an enormous leap. Flint looked down at his own body. Its transformation was less physical than Maroney's. His limbs hadn't stretched. *Not yet, anyway.* Placing the right palm of his hand on the flat wall, he noticed a change. A suction against the sheer concrete. One of the wildlife biologists at the station, who had taken a sabbatical in Brazil to study amphibians and warm up, had told him how geckos moved. Their toes were covered in microscopic hairs, which generated Van der Waals forces that allowed them to stick to smooth surfaces.

Feeling resistance as he placed his hand on the wall, he tried a similar motion with his bare foot. It stuck to the wall, even as he pushed up.

The joy Flint felt at this new physical capacity, after years of disabling arthritis, was tempered by a stab of profound loss. After a moment, Flint identified the source of this conflicting emotion.

I should be in the pasture, feeding the city. I'm letting the hive down.

He ignored the impulse and, hand over hand, began to climb the pasture wall. *They should write a movie about me. Gecko Boy in the Alien Ice Dome.*

As Flint reached the summit of the wall, he guessed he was about halfway from the center of the dome to its edge. Now, as he walked, he noticed how different his bare feet felt on the cool concrete below. It was like wearing spikes on a rubberized track. He was in harmony with his environment. If only he could build and harvest.

No. The door. I'm opening the door.

When the urge to stop, to perform some vital hive task almost overwhelmed him, Flint thought about the ice. He latched onto a memory of a vast plain of ice, the curve of Mount Erebus in the distance.

A few minutes later, the hair on the back of Flint's neck began to prickle. This was a human feeling, not an alien one, and he began to suspect he was being followed. The whisper of a threat grew more powerful, but Flint couldn't see anyone when he swiveled his head. The corridors around him were empty, and when he moved through the gaps between buildings and inspected the rooftops, no one was there.

Staring at the glow of moss on top of one of the hexagonal city towers, Flint noticed a faint movement. *Is someone watching from the roof?* But no, the movement was more distant, like dust or a shooting star. Squinting, Flint looked out past the edge of the rooftop. As he recognized the source of the movement, his stomach churned, his brain rejecting the sheer *wrongness* of the motion.

Hundreds of feet above him, at a distance he never would have been able to see a few days ago, someone was climbing along the underside of the dome. As he stared up, the figure froze, but Flint could still see it. The person was staring right at him.

Maroney. It has to be Maroney. The hive lord sent a drone to find the flute.

Cursing under his breath, Flint ran into the nearest building. They had his location now, and soon Maroney would drop down to the nearest terminal and tell Wulf and Adams where to find him. Triangulating with the gel pool and his present location, they'd find him almost immediately.

Inaction would doom him to capture, so Flint forced himself to move his feet. He worked to find covered passageways through the city, avoiding the open gaps between buildings where Maroney would be able to spot him. Soon, though, the available corridors petered out, and he found himself forced to cross twenty feet of open space between buildings. He was near the edge of the dome now, and the synthetic structures were fewer and farther between, dotted among circular moss pastures and open space.

The open ground, glowing pale blue, was ominous, and making a split-second decision, Flint doubled back through the building, working his way back toward the center of the dome. Moving fast on unfamiliar ground, he stumbled but stopped his fall with the faintest brush of his fingers against the smooth concrete of the nearby wall. Thinking about the newfound friction of his fingers, he had an idea. Hanging onto his memory of Mount Erebus, he accessed what he knew about the architecture of the city. It wasn't a perfect solution, but if he could find his way into a maintenance tunnel, he'd have a chance.

It took a few minutes of searching, but after looking through a dozen rooms, Flint found a dark maintenance shaft that headed deeper.

Here goes nothing.

The stench of rotten meat riding the breeze out of the narrow shaft caught him off guard as he stepped onto the ladder and began his descent.

CHAPTER 37

When Eva reached the platform that circumscribed the city, she looked out at the skyline and shivered, hope for her people mingling with a sense of alarm as she stared at the tall central tower that threatened to destroy Earth.

She felt exposed here, on the wide-open rim of the dome. Well. There was no way around it. If they found her, they found her.

The problem now was she had no idea which of the exterior airlocks Flint was headed to. There were six along the exterior of the dome, built at even intervals, but she'd been unconscious so many times inside the dome that she had no idea which one was which. The buildings and moss-filled wells that dotted the rim of the dome were symmetrical, and they gave her no clue about her destination.

I'll have to check them one at a time.

She might be able to find the information she needed at one of the access terminals, but she didn't want to risk alerting Adams and Wulf about what she was up to. She'd have to take them in turn and hope she could tell which airlock would open onto the backside for the Navy.

Running at the fastest clip she could maintain for any length of time, she reached the first airlock within minutes, inspecting the round circle of a door for clues. Fortunately, it was covered with a thin layer of what looked like dust. *Spores. From the moss.* Eva abandoned it and continued to run.

The next door was covered in a similar dust. Eva ran her finger through it, disappointed. When she turned back to head to the rim, she heard a voice from somewhere she couldn't identify. No. Not a voice. She was picking up information with her new sensory organs. Emotions. Rusty orange disapproval.

The blinking red of annoyance. And a deep indigo pit of loss and longing. As a dun silhouette emerged from murky obscurity and squirmed into focus, Eva connected the source of the voice.

Fucking Wulf. Or whoever he is now. Her stomach turned.

Now, he spoke in audible words.

"What's your game here, Evie? Can't you see the shining hand of fate? We were together a million years ago on another planet, and we were together ten years ago on Earth. Let's do it again. For really, really old times' sake."

"You're a bastard."

"Who, me? I'm a changed man."

As Wulf said the words, he laughed, and the tendrils at his throat vibrated like gelatin.

Eva wanted to chuckle, but she also wanted to vomit. She couldn't deny they shared a certain connection. Without the persistent invisible thread between them, she couldn't hate him as much as she did.

He can help me get the flute back.

An idea occurred to her.

"We need more help to find Flint. To find the flute," she said.

"I've got that drone on the dome scanning for him. We know where he's going. It's just a matter of time before we pin that fly to the cork."

"The city is large and Maroney can't hold on up there forever. We should let the Navy in. We can pod them and use them to help us. We'll need more drones."

"As you have demonstrated, the gel isn't perfect. It takes time for the memories to embed, for physical changes to dominate the host."

Eva stared down at her long limbs.

"Where's Adams?" she said.

"Headed to the tower to calibrate the radiation. He belongs at the heart of the city."

She purred, imbuing her voice with amber waves of reassurance, a sparkle of scarlet seduction.

"Come on. Let's get one airlock of sailors in the pods. Just one. They can marinate for a week. Two weeks. Months if we have to. Let's just try it. If we fail, we can do things your way."

She felt a wave of wariness wash over her, but Wulf's longing overpowered it. She tried to tamp down on a flash of victory, but not before Wulf noticed it.

"You always could win an argument. Fine. We'll try it your way. I'm sick of having no one but Adams to talk to, anyway."

They walked along the rim of the dome in silence. Eva resisted the urge to put distance between herself and Wulf. She barely had a plan, after all.

When they reached the next airlock, Eva's breath caught. There was no spore dust on the wide circular door, and small drops of water had beaded on the floor. Near the edges of the room were stray gray threads. She felt a sudden wave of fear as she remembered how they had encircled and choked her in the submersible.

Wulf stuck his hands in a small circle of gel near an access panel.

"There are two submersibles and four divers outside. What do you think? Bring in the divers and crush the subs like Coke cans?"

CHAPTER 38

THE MAINTENANCE TUNNELS WERE cramped, and Flint was forced to crawl. Still, he made good time, and soon he emerged into one of the circular gel refining rooms. Looking up, he saw four moss collection shafts, each of which would carry the harvest from one of the pastures along the exterior of the dome to this refining pond. There were dozens of these throughout the city, he knew, each serving a handful of pastures. He stared at the identical outlets for a moment, before choosing the one he thought would take him closest to the edge of the dome. The gray matte collection shafts were smooth, smoother than the concrete, and Flint prayed they weren't made from some sort of no-friction alien material. Climbing onto the edge of the gel pool, he placed his palm on a shaft interior.

There was just enough surface roughness there for the small hooks on his skin to catch. Flint edged along the side of the pool to get the best possible grip, then set his feet and jumped. His chest hit the edge of the outlet with a sharp rap, but his hands caught the interior surface, and he strained his back muscles until he could wiggle up into the chute. Bracing his hands and feet, he began to inch himself up.

When he reached the top of the tube, he'd have to cover a few hundred feet to get to the airlock. He hoped Maroney would be too focused on the surface exits of the building to see him, but it was a possibility. Flint understood Maroney's instincts because he understood his own. The primary drives were to build and feed the city. But in the face of a threat to the hive, Maroney might attack him.

If Maroney attacked him, he could always retreat back into his drone instincts. *Picking moss and putting up alien drywall. Just how I wanted to spend the first two hundred years of my retirement.*

As the light in the tunnel brightened, signaling he was approaching the outlet, he decided he would move as fast as he could and hope for the best.

And he would keep a firm grip on his knife. Just in case.

BORED OF WATCHING WULF use the terminal and tired of looking at his idiotic face, Eva went back out and looked over the rim, down at the glowing city. It was impossibly alien and it was home. The conflicting emotions the view inspired almost made her turn away until she noticed a pinprick of movement near the bottom of her vision, in one of the wide circular depressions she now understood as a primary food source for the city.

Astonished, she watched as Flint crawled out of a small circular well in the middle of the pasture, place a large knife on its edge, and begin to pick handfuls of glowing moss. His movements were calculated, repetitive, and elegant.

What is he doing? She thought about her own role in her city on the other world. She'd been a scientist. She and her team had shared a specialized diet, intended to boost intellectual capacity, dull the sharper pheromonal emotions, and increase brain connectivity. But there had been others, too. The drones.

Her mind resisted the word, briefly. Her human brain understood it as something negative, an insult. But in her other half, it was positive. A vital organ in the organism.

He was warring with his alien instincts as much as her. Swiveling her head, she saw Wulf was still absorbed in his work. She needed to get Flint's attention without alerting Wulf.

Sometimes, the simplest solution was the best. Reaching down to one of the troughs of glowing moss that lined the platform, she yanked out a tuft and lobbed it at Flint's head, hoping her new alien capabilities included a powerful throwing arm.

The moss connected, and Flint looked up at her. At first, his face was confused, blank, but soon emotion returned to his face. She thought he was Flint again. More or less.

"What are you doing?" Wulf asked from behind her. His voice was inky gray with suspicion. Eva plucked another handful of moss and lobbed it, this time at Wulf's stupid face.

"Moss fight?"

Wulf strode over and peered out into the city.

Flint had disappeared.

"Knock it off. We don't need to tear up the grass in our new home."

Eva moved to smooth out the moss, and as she did, her eyes flicked downward. Flint was there, flattened against the wall, clinging just below the rim. *I guess we all got some new skills.* His knife was clutched in his teeth.

Sometimes, the simplest solution is the best.

"Look at that!" she said, striding over to the edge of the rim and pointing toward the enormous building in the center.

Wulf, annoyed, strode over and looked in the direction she was pointing. As he did, Eva kicked his feet out from under him, sending him toppling over the rim. He landed with a thump in the moss and she grabbed Flint's hand, pulling him up beside her.

"I'll let Ash in. Keep Wulf entertained," she said.

As Flint scrambled up, Eva's leg brushed something. A powerful wave of emotion overtook her.

The flute.

Mindlessly, with the urgency of an addict, she reached for it. clawing at the waistband of Flint's under-suit and punching him as he tried to bat her searching hands away.

"Stop!" Flint said.

"You bitch!" Wulf shouted, his voice barely reaching her from over the rim. The harsh, human notes pulled Eva back into her body.

Wulf wanted her to get the flute. He wanted her to take it up to Adams at the tower. Wulf thought if they could fire off the antenna, he could rule the Earth. What an idiot. He didn't understand the situation at all. She couldn't give him what he wanted.

With tremendous effort, Eva pulled her hand away and ran toward the terminal, plunging her hand into the bowl-sized pool of gel at its side. Swiftly, she sent out lightning-fast commands to stop the threads worming their way to the divers and their submersibles. As they retreated back into the dome, she sent a single, clear command.

Open the door.

CHAPTER 39

The instant Eva saw the cilia on the door crawl and ripple, she spun and ran toward the rim of the platform. Below her, Wulf squared off against Flint. Wulf was taller, but Flint had a knife. They moved warily, flattening a circle of moss at their feet as they danced in a tight arc.

When Wulf moved, he shot like lightning, the spurs near his wrists driving toward Flint's face. Flint turned his head in time for the blow to deflect off his eyebrow, but it left a nasty gash, and blinking the blood out of his eye left him a half-second behind. As Flint scrambled back across the pasture ground, his fist clenched around a handful of moss. Pulling it free, he dabbed at his eye while Wulf regained his feet. With the moss in his right hand, Flint was disoriented, the knife limp by his side. Eva knew he couldn't block another blow.

She made a split-second decision and ran, leaping over the edge of the pasture, praying as she sailed the thirty feet down that her new body wouldn't simply shatter against the ground.

But she had aimed true, spinning in the air so she hit Wulf in the chest with her shoulder bone. She heard a crack, and an inhuman cry of pain that activated an ancient alien memory in her brain so powerful that for several moments, she couldn't breathe.

That was the sound I heard when he laid our first brood.

The part of her that was Eva nearly choked with laughter at the thought of Wulf, narcissist extraordinaire, giving birth to a child.

Laying an egg isn't the same. Much easier.

Wulf cried again, crushed under Eva's body, and she rolled off him, pushing his head back into the moss with a hand against his throat.

He coughed and choked.

"You're going to fail as a mother twice? You've abandoned Sophie and now you're going to leave our brood in the emptiness of space. Our family can live again, Eva. You can have a second chance."

His eyes glittered with tears for a moment, before translucent eyelids slid down and cleared them away.

Eva might have given in then. She had led a lonely life for years, her shame at being discovered stealing Roman coins isolating her from her colleagues. She was ashamed about her relationship with Wulf and ashamed of leaving her daughter.

Instead, she was distracted by the sound of rubber soles on concrete and looked up at the rim walk to find five assault rifles pointed down into the pasture. Two were pointed straight at her.

The soldiers were wearing aquamarine environmental suits, their heads encased in clear domes beaded with water from the airlock. The droplets swam with bioluminescent algae, and the faint glow illuminated the HAB tactical security team's fear and adrenaline. Eva was reminded of the disgust she'd felt when she caught the first glance of her own transformation.

She was a monster now, and so was Flint. Staring at the dark wells of the gun barrels, Eva realized the military might simply shoot them. She moved to hold up her hands, then felt ashamed of their transformed shapes. She left them by her sides, brushing against the silvery fabric that stretched over her lengthened limbs.

"It's me, Eva," she said. "Doctor Eva Ward."

Wulf moaned on the ground beneath her, rustling faintly. Eva guessed she had broken his ribs.

"If you twitch, I shoot." The voice was that of Captain Sanchez.

Eva took a shallow breath. Out of the corner of her eye, she saw Flint reach for the ground. What was he doing?

"Drop it!" The tip of Captain Sanchez's gun twitched ever so slightly. "Come on, Flint."

A flutter of movement and a tuft of moss floated to the ground, twirled by one of the dome's soft breezes.

"Don't shoot him. He's not in his right mind," Eva said, holding her body like a statue. Suddenly conscious of her own movements, she felt a fierce itch creep up along the stretched skin around her calves. *Growing pains.*

"I think we should shoot them, Captain." This male voice, a half step behind the captain, was shaky.

"We're all still here. We've just got company. The person Flint's sharing his brain with was a worker in the city. I think he has a strong instinctual drive to harvest. But he came here to let you in. We both did. We can help the subs outside the dock. We can help you understand this place. We're talking about a civilization that was able to preserve its memories for millions of years. Imagine what we could learn here. Imagine how human technology could advance. Communications. Material science. Medicine."

"Sure. You're all ready to play in the next Earth versus the Universe basketball tournament," Captain Sanchez said.

The itching around her knees became more insistent. Eva tried to ignore it. For the first time, she wondered what her life might look like after she got out of the dome. Where her hopes and dreams should be, however, there was just an empty space. No part of her believed she would ever leave this place.

She was fragmented, a failure on two fronts, and totally alone.

"Adams is in the tower at the center of the city. You have to stop him from firing off the antenna."

As she said this, she closed her eyes, sure she was about to be riddled with bullets. This time, no one would carry her to a pod. The darkness behind her eyelids whorled with pinpricks of light. She heard a whoosh of air, like the sound of a diving bird.

When the rifle fired, she flinched and fell to her knees, certain the agonized bellow echoing off the dense gray walls of the dome must be her own.

But no, there was no pain, no sensation at all, and she opened her eyes to chaotic, many-limbed movement.

Maroney.

The whoosh she had heard was Maroney dropping from the ceiling of the dome, a dive-bombing death angel. He had landed on the sailor behind the captain's right shoulder, and the man was a crumpled heap. Now, he threw wild punches at the intruders. Knocking the barrel of one sailor's rifle several inches to the left, he diverted a loud shot straight into another sailor's hip. The man screamed. When he dropped the weapon, he was so shocked he seemed surprised by the sound of the metal clattering against the ground.

Sanchez spun, tracking Maroney's loping strides with her gun barrel. She took aim, and Eva thought her shot would probably hit. Both halves of her mind raced and came to the same conclusion.

I can't keep fighting myself. She reached for the million-year-old knowledge she needed, took an enormous breath, and willed her throat to make the necessary sounds.

STOP!

The sound that left her throat was not a word in English, but the million-year-old command of a hive queen to a drone, a call to action that warned the drones of a lethal threat. All hands on deck. As the sound left her throat, Eva felt a synergistic pride, a feeling that the two halves of herself had merged. Eva's alien jockey was no longer trying to destroy her. It needed her. It didn't understand these people, these weapons, this language. She felt a great sense of pride as Maroney stilled and stood, ears cocked, neck exposed so he could sense maximum information about her plan. As he did, Captain Sanchez breathed, aimed, and fired a shot into the center of his forehead.

Given Maroney's willowy limbs, there was a certain lightness to his fall, but when he thumped onto the ground, he looked as dead as the soldier next to him. Eva screamed again, and waves of pulsing yellow ricocheted across the roof of the dome. Captain Sanchez stared blankly at her, but near Eva's feet, Wulf wailed.

The captain's nostrils flared as she looked at the enemy's fallen body.

"Is that Adams? You said he was in the tower."

Flint coughed, and as Eva moved her head toward him, she saw his fist clench.

"That was Bugsy Maroney. The cook of the *Bethany Rose*."

"What the fuck?" The soldier's voice was barely audible from Eva's position at the bottom of the pasture.

"Why did you shoot him? He would have obeyed me!" Eva said. Sanchez turned, and looked down at Eva.

"Even if that's true, how am I supposed to trust you?"

"He built this city, and he was alone here for two hundred years," Flint said, his voice raspy with anger. "He saved Eva's life. In many ways, he saved his entire civilization."

"I'm sorry," Sanchez said. To her credit, she sounded sincere. "But we are in operationally idiosyncratic terrain here. And he attacked my squad." She glanced down at her wounded man, attended by a squad mate.

"Is he alive?" Sanchez asked.

"Not for long," the soldier providing first aid replied. His voice was clipped.

"If you put him in the pods, he'll live," Eva said. "There's a gel down here. It has incredible regenerative properties."

The captain looked from Eva to Flint to Wulf, eyes flickering with disgust as her gaze scanned across their mutated bodies.

"Some prices are too high to pay," she said. "We'll stay with Evans as long as we need to, and then we'll go get Adams."

CHAPTER 40

Maroney's limp body agitated Flint. It was shameful it was still unattended, and Flint's arms and hands twitched as he stared at the old sailor. The captain, noticing his agitation, trained her rifle on him. "Whatever you're thinking about trying, don't," she said.

Flint's brows creased inward, and red flashed across his eyes.

"You'll leave him to rot in the city he built? He deserves a place of honor."

"You want to bury him?" Sanchez asked. Her voice was wary.

"The people of this city do not bury their dead. Their bodies are recycled into the community."

Swift footsteps approached the rim.

"Do whatever you want with the freak, but there's no fucking way you're eating Evans," one of the soldiers said.

Flint, jolted back into his humanity, felt briefly revolted. A faint breeze flowed across his skin, which rose up in goosebumps.

"I'm not planning on making meatballs," he said. "I just want to return him to the gel."

"What exactly does that mean?" Sanchez asked.

Flint took a breath. "It means I'm going to carry his body over to that well and drop him in a chute that will carry him down to a digesting pit. It's how we get our food, yes, but also our fertilizers, our medicine."

"Let's just shoot these freaks," Sanchez's man said, his voice breaking into a higher octave. Flint saw the young sailor's gun shake.

"Please. It's my job," Flint said. "You're judging things on human terms."

Finally, Sanchez relented. Pale blue relief washed across Flint's field of vision as he climbed up to the rim, cradled Maroney's body in his arms and leaped back onto the moss. As he released the old sailor's body into the chute, tears welled in his eyes. He was startled as a set of new eyelids shot down to sweep them away.

"His work is done," he announced as he turned back around.

"His work is done," Eva echoed. He wasn't sure, but he thought he'd heard Wulf echo the words, too. In the gel, the last chemical signals of Maroney's body would spread through the city. He would linger, briefly, in the network of information and emotions. Eventually, after the gel recognized his flesh was dead and began to break him down, he would nourish the city he had built, returning to the moss. It was beautiful. The alien civilization's treatment of death was...well, not humane, Flint supposed. Or maybe it *was* more humane than locking death under stones behind graveyard fences. In a living hive, the city would feel the loss together.

Including Adams, who must now know they were coming. If he was preparing the antenna, he would have noticed the airlock open. He would be able to feel Maroney's death.

Backing away from the well, Flint climbed up to the edge of the rim, glancing down at the wounded soldier on the platform. The one who had been shot in the hip had taken his helmet off—what was the point, with a bullet hole through his suit—and pressed his blood-smeared hands against the wound.

"Let me dock the subs. Is there a medic with them?" Flint said. Captain Sanchez, breathing hard, nodded.

"Do it."

ULTIMATELY, THIRTEEN PEOPLE MADE their way inside the dome. A team medic stayed behind with Evans and Wulf, plus a two-man guard.

When the airlock opened the final time, Eva was surprised to see Rear Admiral Ash among the sailors. She wondered if the same impulse that had driven her and

Flint here had gotten to him, too. He was as contained and alert as always, and the only one among his men who Eva noticed taking in the vista of the city.

Flint and Eva had their own guards now, well-armed shadows whose eyes stayed superglued to their movements through the corridors of the city. As a group, they made slow progress. They were soldiers in enemy territory, although there was no one in the city to fight. As they marched, Ash interrogated her about the materials of the antenna. Much of Eva's newfound scientific knowledge was stored in an alien language, and she translated through English as best she could.

"You have to understand, I'm a biologist, not an engineer," she said.

"I thought you were an archaeologist."

She was quiet for a moment.

"I was a biologist, too. A long time ago."

His head swiveled and he stared at her, his eyes piercing the clear material of his environmental suit.

"So. Who's in control now?" he asked.

"I am," Eva said, pressing her mouth shut until he looked away. Their footsteps echoed in the silence until they came to a break between buildings. Ash held up a hand signal and his men stopped cold. Two of them, marching near the back under heavy packs, circled around him, whispering to one another in quiet voices. Eva couldn't hear them, but she could feel their emotions a little. Conflict in the service of a common goal. One of them kept glancing over at her and Flint. Finally, Ash approached.

"Operationally, do you think we should climb up and take down the antenna, or should we bring down the tower from the base?"

Eva closed her eyes and thought for a moment. The answer, when it came to her, was startling.

"The tower is the antenna. The controls are at the top, but it runs up the whole length of the building."

Ash nodded.

"Then let's take it down at the base. That way, we won't have to risk fighting our way up the staircase."

Faint movement along the ground distracted Eva. At first, she thought it was a change in the quality of light from the glowing moss that lined the corridors. Soon, however, she realized the moss was vibrating, faintly at first, throwing its glow in weird vibrational waves across the corridor walls and floor. The noise and shaking grew, and Ash's men fell into a defensive ring.

Ash seized Eva's neck, the rubber of his gloves digging into the soft tendrils there. She made a mewling noise as he held her gaze.

"What's going on?"

There was a rustle from the side, and then Flint knocked into Ash's hand with a defensive rattle.

"Don't touch her!" Flint said, then backed off as four rifle barrels turned on him. Eva coughed and touched her neck. She saw the disgust on Ash's face as he looked at the tendrils at her throat. She opened her mouth and was about to answer Ash's question when a tremendous crack answered it for him.

The tower was shaking. The entire building was spiraling upward, slowly but unmistakably. Eva stared up at the top of the dome, barely managing to see a faint movement in the distance.

"I thought you said he couldn't set off the antenna without the flute?" Ash said, then paused and grabbed the radio at his hip. He pressed a button.

"Ash for rim camp. Come in, rim camp." His voice was nearly drowned out by the rumbling of the tower behind him. Specks of dust, a mix of concrete flakes and moss spores, began to fall from the sky.

There was no answer. Eva put her hand out, letting the falling dust collect on her skin like snowflakes as the radio's silence seemed to suck all hope from Ash's expression. A flicker of movement caught her eye as she stared at his face. Something odd in the reflection of his helmet. It was a long, thin body.

Wulf.

Eva barely had time to turn around as Wulf barreled down the hallway at lightning speed, grabbed her around the waist, and pulled her into the open space between buildings. A moment later, he twisted and tumbled down an open hatch, and darkness swallowed them both.

CHAPTER 41

Wulf had captured Eva so quickly there was nothing anyone could do. Time froze as Flint stared at the upward movement of the tower, the roar of the rising antenna filling the dome. He knew what would happen next: a hole would open in the roof of the dome, and the antenna would release a powerful acid that could melt anything on this planet, including solid rock. The mechanism would burn a hole in the ice, clearing the way for the antenna that would turn Earth into a planet of alien slaves.

How much longer would he be able to hold onto his own mind? Where was Wulf taking Eva?

If he ran to the tower now, he might be able to hook into one of the portals and reverse the antenna's movement. He might be able to save the precious Antarctica ice shelf.

But then Eva might die. And he had grown fond of the acerbic archaeologist. Doubly so now, considering their alien link.

A lawnmower-sized chunk of concrete smashed onto the ground twenty feet in front of Flint, breaking his reverie. He thought about the ice shelf above him, cold and persistent.

And then he sprinted after Eva. Ash could try and shoot him, but he was going to save her.

It took him five minutes of running to find the hatch into the sub-dome tunnels. Ripping it open, Flint ignored the small frictional surfaces along the side he could have used as handholds, and leaped straight down. Fifteen feet down, he slammed into hard concrete. The only way out was a horizontal shaft with an opening so small he was forced to crawl. He held his breath and wiggled his way in. *Where is Wulf taking her?*

The tunnel split out into a tomblike antechamber, which fed into what looked like a laboratory. This one was more advanced than anything he'd seen in the city. Moving as silently as possible, he lingered behind the doorway to listen for information. After a moment, he leaned his head back too, experimenting with retrieving emotional information from the small tendrils of his neck.

Longing. Overwhelming longing. As Flint listened to their conversation, he began to understand.

"I brought you here to show you something," Wulf said, low and pleading.

"Get it through your thick, alien-infested skull. We are done."

There were two thick thumping footsteps and a tremendous crash. Wulf shouted in pain.

"If you want to kill me after I show you why I brought you here, fine. Just give me one minute. Please. Let me show you, our child."

Flint heard Eva gasp and risked sticking his head around the door. Eva and Wulf were backlit by a glow from a gel tube. This one was larger than the others Flint had seen, and his alien instincts told him he was in something like an intensive care unit.

When he looked at the tube, he understood. Inside floated the body of Lieutenant Kim. Except that wasn't quite right. The body wasn't Kim's. It was almost entirely transformed, more than Flint's or Eva's, or even Maroney's. Only certain lines of the face remained.

So this is what we used to look like. The alien was beautiful, with elegant spider limbs and a curving thorax, the neck alive with sensory tendrils, the hands double-jointed. The alien's skin rippled with subcutaneous ink, like that of an octopus.

"She's dead," Eva said.

"No, she's our daughter. She's going to live again."

"I meant Kim." Eva's voice was reproachful.

Wulf shrugged and stared back through the tube.

"That water is thirty-two degrees. Maybe colder. She was perfectly preserved. With her organ function stopped, the gel had time to acquire information about human cell generation, growth, and chemical processing. Her memories are being rebuilt from the stalk up. She will be the best of us, Eva. And now you have to help me get that flute away from Flint."

Wulf turned, then rotated his body toward his location. Flint ducked back behind the doorway, but he knew it was too late. He'd already felt the eyes on him. Wulf had known he would follow. How could he not? He was their drone, after all.

"Give me the flute!" Wulf's command was unmistakable, and Flint found himself rising back through the tunnel, his instinct to obey moving his legs upward. Wulf was still standing by the tank, his ruddy, silver hair lit gold by the glow from the tank behind him. Flint reached into his waistband and grabbed the small cylinder wrapped there. He approached Wulf slowly, at first. Then, when he was six feet away, he clenched his fist around the hilt of the knife in his waistband, ran past Wulf, and plunged it into the tank where Kim's regenerated body floated.

The blade almost failed to penetrate the rubbery material of the tube, but Flint used the force of the momentum to pull downward. However Maroney had changed, he had kept his knife sharp, and despite the resistance from the material, Flint made a hole large enough for gel to begin streaming onto the concrete floor. Eva and Wulf wailed in unison.

"She's not done yet. She'll die without the gel!" Wulf's voice, undergirded by pitch-black, pulsing waves of sorrow, dropped Flint to the ground with the force of emotion, and he writhed there.

"I'll cut your fucking throat out!" Wulf shouted, a curse followed by a chirping threat Flint barely managed to wrap his head around as alien profanity. He hoped he would live long enough to give a linguistics grad student some exceptional thesis material.

But Wulf was on top of him now and delivered two choking punches to Flint's throat before Eva grabbed his arm to stop him. He kicked her away and she yelped in pain.

"If you can get our daughter into another tube, she might survive," Eva shouted.

Wulf looked down at the crumpled body on the floor, and Eva was nearly knocked back by crimson fury.

"You would kill our child rather than be with me?"

He turned on her now, kicking the lieutenant's corpse to the side and moving, keeping his center of gravity low as he crawled across the ground toward Eva. As he moved, Eva saw Flint rise from the floor and follow him, stepping where he stepped, mimicking his movements to disguise the noise. Wulf's body shifted back a little, a final coil before he struck. As he did, Flint's arm snuck around his neck and cut, delivering a hard, sharp slash between the coiling tendrils there.

Wulf's face contorted in pain and his mouth flew open, but all that emerged was a rasping gurgle. Red blood and a second fluid, a thick amber goo, flowed from his throat. His neck tendrils waved like sea grass in the mingling fluids.

Flint wiped down his knife on the leg of his under-suit and looked at Eva.

"I'm sorry," he said. "I know you wanted to do that yourself."

"Never look a gift horse in the oozing throat," she said, forced after a moment to look away from Wulf's limp body.

The overwhelming grinding noise that had punished their eardrums since the tower moved suddenly crescendoed, cutting off whatever response Flint might have made to her weak joke.

Particles of concrete fell from the ceiling. If the antenna hadn't reached the roof, it was close.

The only thing left was to stop Adams. Eva wondered if it was even possible. They were both pheromonally susceptible to him. And with the plans so near completion, Flint might succumb to the power of the flute. An idea began to form in her mind. The antenna tower would churn through the rock and ice above it with the help of some kind of superheated acid spray. Highly toxic and dense, the acid was stored in deep cisterns below the city. It could dissolve anything on Earth and most things on her home planet.

She grabbed Flint's arm. They didn't have to stop Adams. They just had to cut off his fuel line.

Eva pulled Flint close. She tried shouting her plan to him, but even six inches away, it was hopeless in the bone-rattling noise. Instead, she placed the palm of her hand against Flint's throat, hoping he would pick up what she was putting down.

Trust me.

He nodded, and she spun and led the way to the nearby access shaft.

There were no handholds, no ladder, just rough surfaces on the sides of the tube they could use to lower themselves down into the pit of the Earth. Eva felt the pressure change in her head as she descended. *At least I know I still have an inner ear.* The light grew dimmer and dimmer. There was no moss down here, but the concrete glowed faintly with geo-microbic effects.

Flint was climbing above her. If he slipped, he would knock her off the wall, but her worries diminished as they went down, the steady movements of his hands and legs comforting. Finally, the shaft ended, and Eva walked out onto a dark, smooth concrete floor.

The ceilings were low, and the wall behind her curved. It was so bright so suddenly that her eyes revolted, but after a minute of blinking, she began to take in her surroundings. She was in a large, donut-shaped room. Functional and low-ceilinged, it enclosed a large open space, in which floated something that looked like a small sun.

Perhaps ten feet high, the liquid orb hovered, its surface the color of magma. Arcs of plasma shot off the surface.

This was the energy source on which her people had built their civilization.

How is it loose? she thought, then noticed a faint glimmer around the acid ball's exterior, distorting the air. A force field?

It's not a force field. It's a distortion in the light. A hyper-dense object in the center is creating localized microgravity. Flint drew up beside her, eyes wide with anxiety. If they released the ball, the acid would drop, flowing through the floor, through the lower surface of the dome, and into the Earth's core. She glanced at the cylinder rolled into Flint's waistband.

"We have to destroy the flute," she said.

Flint's hand went to his waist, and he clutched the instrument through the fabric.

"It's our only hope," he said.

"We made it through a million years of space and time," she said. "Someday, we'll try again." In an infinite universe on an infinite time scale, anything was possible.

Eva held out her hand. "Let me play one last song."

She imbued her voice with signals of compassion, but also unyielding command. Flint placed the flute in her palm, in a hand that was now perfectly suited to the instrument it held. She hadn't been particularly musical in either of her past lives, but now she held the flute to her lips and played a simple tone. The tendrils on Flint's throat rose to attention, and she played a song of mourning for her people. A million years ago, every person in the hive would have joined in. They were not a solitary species, and the lonely tones of the flute in an empty room nearly ripped her heart out.

When she couldn't stand it any longer, she dropped the cylinder of bone from her lips, walked toward the acid, and flung the flute inside. As the microgravity caught it and arcs of acid licked against it, the material sizzled and disappeared. The city around them would stay dead, a stillborn shell. Eva turned and found a nearby terminal, a six-foot high cylinder with two displays and an access pool full of gel. She raised an eyebrow at Flint.

"I'm going to release the acid and destroy the city. I don't know if we'll make it out."

He nodded.

"We should climb. Try to find Adams. He's the last of our kind. He shouldn't end things alone."

THE FALL OF THE acid into the Earth was one of the most terrifying things Flint had ever seen. He was a geologist, accustomed to thinking about rock and ice on a scale of thousands of years. Rock wasn't eternal, but it changed very, very slowly.

The acid dissolved the floor of the room so rapidly Flint barely saw it. There was no splash, but simply a hole in the Earth that registered on his retinae instantaneously. Then Eva grabbed his arm and they were climbing up through the shaft.

When they reached the level of the city, they found the grinding ascent of the antenna had stopped.

Just as well. It's a dead thing now that the key is gone.

They paused for only a moment, after which heat began to rise from the shaft they had just exited. Eva held her hand over the opening, then drew it away in alarm, raising an eyebrow at Flint. He looked at his feet.

"When we released that acid, we bored a hole into the center of the Earth. We've created a pressure release. I'm not surprised we're seeing volcanic activity now."

Eva's jaw opened, and Flint pushed past her, searching for an access point into the tower. In the end, they had to climb the sheer sides for thirty feet to a circular window, after which they were able to find the stairs. They moved upward in silence, and Flint tried to enjoy the painless physical motion of his own body.

I'm in the best shape of my life. He choked down an ironic laugh and kept moving upward. When they reached the roof, it was so changed that he was briefly disoriented. There was no vista of the city now. Instead, the door at the top of the dome had started to open. The cilia of the door had flowed outward to surround the perimeter, twisting together into gray cords, stretching upward into the rock. It was like being trapped in a cable bundle. A gust of cold air rattled Flint's teeth, and he wrapped his long limbs around himself.

I thought I would die on the ice. At least I can die under it.

The access panel on the roof was still there, and as Flint and Eva made their way toward it, they heard weeping. In the dim light of the cavern, it took Flint a moment to make out the collapsed shape of Adams's body.

As Flint leaned over him, Adams pointed a thin, accusing finger.

"You killed us! You killed an entire civilization. It's genocide."

"It was going to be genocide either way," Eva said.

"We're here now," Flint added. "The last of the hive."

He reached down and grasped Adams's hand in his own, the joints of the fingers locking together like puzzle pieces. Eva stayed standing, then put a hand on the ceiling, against the enormous gray area of the door. Flint followed her gaze. The doors of the dome were dynamic. Flint considered what Eva had told him about being snatched from her submarine. The cilia there were clearly advanced. She looked at him.

"When I entered the airlock, I came in a pod. Maybe we can reverse engineer the cilia to take us back out into the open and send us to the surface."

Flint considered this, wondering what sort of life support systems the threads were capable of. Filled with gel, he thought they might make it.

"Can you do it from that station?" he asked. Eva plunged her hands into the gel and stared at the blinking screen.

"Yes," she said. "But—"

"What?" Flint asked.

"Maybe it's better if we go down with the dome. Even if we get out, what kind of life will we have?"

It was a risk. He certainly didn't think he'd be returning to geology research on the ice.

As he was thinking, the roof dropped half a foot, and a jet of steam streamed out of the stairwell.

No time to ruminate.

"We are our people's memory," Flint said. "Do it. Adams too. It's not genocide just yet."

He directed this last statement at the body on the floor.

Eva nodded, and the screen of her workstation began to flash with ideograms and lines of code. As the heat around them grew, tendrils descended from the ceiling of the dome. Before, Flint would have found it terrifying, but he more or less understood their function. As they wrapped around him, the cotton candy threads knitting, filling his eyes and lungs, he was plunged into blackness. Soon, a soporific calm took over, and he lost consciousness.

CHAPTER 42

Antarctica's volcanic event caused a hundred feet of ground subsidence. The research station there, evacuated by the Navy, cracked into pieces as the ground beneath it bucked and sank.

Fifteen Navy SEALs were lost in what was reported by the United States government as accidental deaths during an unforeseen incident on a submarine participating in war games.

In the hold of the U.S.S. *Taft*, Flint was locked in a reinforced cell. What he assumed was three times a day, a six-inch-thick plexiglass airlock opened and delivered a meal. Flint could not see nor hear anything beyond the walls of his cell. He also couldn't obtain any pheromonal information. It was possible his senses were gone, but more likely that his prison had been hermetically sealed.

He kept track of the number of meals he'd been served by scratching small tick marks into the wall of his cell. Sometime after he scratched the thirtieth line, something miraculous happened.

The door opened.

Flint almost wept when he saw the face of the woman who entered the room. It was Dr. Milroy.

"How have you been, Doc?"

He watched her face for signs of disgust, but there were none. Only compassion, and also a hint of professional curiosity.

"How are you feeling?" she said.

"Lonely," Flint admitted, staring at the lines on his wall. She looked over and the corner of her mouth twitched in anger.

"How are your hands?" she said.

Flint looked down at his double joints and the protrusion from his wrist bone.

"Pain-free." He coughed in embarrassment. "Are Eva and Adams alive?"

Milroy met his gaze. "Eva is alive. Adams killed himself two weeks ago."

Flint paused to process the news. "Great about Eva, tragic about Adams." A cracking sound echoed from the bones in Flint's neck as he turned to face Milroy. "So, what happens now?"

Milroy's eyebrows perked up. "There's been quite the international kerfuffle since the *Taft* skimmed your pods off the top of the Amundsen Sea. To be honest, several times over the past few weeks, I think the Navy was close to shooting you in your sleep. I tried to come to see you sooner, I promise. They wouldn't let me in. Do you need medical attention? I don't know what I can do, to be honest."

"You just want to poke around in my new guts," Flint said. He didn't blame her. She smiled.

"Maybe," Milroy admitted.

She explained the chaos that ensued after the lava had burned through the alien city. The Navy had lost all communications with Rear Admiral Ash and the other Navy SEALs. They were presumed dead. Before it had been destroyed, the city had sent out a signal to the *Taft* with the approximate location of their pods. He, Eva, and Adams had been cold, almost frozen, but once they'd warmed up they had regained consciousness.

"Why didn't the Navy just kill us?" Flint asked.

"That's the rub. Someone broke the story to the international press. A hacker. He said he'd been tracking the communications. A hacker named Balenciaga or something. Russia accused the United States of using aliens to develop new bioweapons. The only way to fight that accusation is to produce some living aliens."

"Me," Flint said.

"And Eva."

"Is she alright? I mean, really?"

"She spoke to her daughter on the phone yesterday. And apparently, that hacker friend of hers had some clothes delivered in her new size. If you're interested in custom couture..."

Flint stared down at his fatigues, constructed by some crafty bosun.

"So," Flint said. "After much deliberation, the Navy has decided against summary execution. That's nice."

"There's a United Nations ambassador here to welcome you to Earth. Will you see her?"

"You think she'll find it funny if I demand to be taken to her leader?"

Milroy's eyes twinkled, but she shook her head. "She's a serious person. I believe she hopes you will attend some kind of conference."

"Where?" Flint asked. He felt a wary look twist his inhuman face. Visions of somewhere horrible and sweltering swam through his head.

"Reykjavik. Will you go?"

Hot springs. The aurora borealis. And more importantly, glaciers.

Flint nodded. "Send her in. I hear Iceland is lovely this time of year."

About the Author

Ed Downes writes the kind of stories that keep you up past midnight—the suspenseful, the unsettling, and the utterly unputdownable. With a style that blends psychological tension, unexpected twists, and a dash of dread, Ed creates characters who are often one wrong turn from disaster—and readers who can't look away.

His short fiction, including *Qalupalik*, *Regrets*, and *Dr. Bonz*, has been praised for its emotional grit and eerie imagination. *Frozen Echoes* marks his debut novel, and if you hear a faint whisper behind you while reading it... well, that's probably normal.

Ed holds a Master of Fine Arts in Writing Popular Fiction from Seton Hill University, a degree that taught him how to turn nightmares into narrative gold. By day, he's a publishing industry marketing strategist; by night, he's either plotting his next thriller or wondering if the shadows in the hallway just moved.

Originally from Boston, Ed now lives in Raleigh, North Carolina, where he enjoys hiking, fitness, reading, and writing—preferably all at once, when possible. He shares his adventures (literary and otherwise) with his wife Jeanie. You will most likely find him reading or writing thriller fiction or doing fun stuff with his wife Jeanie and two daughters Melissa and Jessica.

Acknowledgements

Writing a novel may be a solitary endeavor, but surviving it certainly isn't. This book would not exist without the support, inspiration, and occasional kick-in-the-pants from the people below.

To my wife, Jeanie—my compass, my confidante, and my best friend. You've always had my back, even when I was too lost in plot twists to say thank you. You're the love behind every chapter.

To my daughters, Melissa and Jessica—you've shown me what unconditional love really looks like. You loved me even when I did not deserve it. That means more than I can ever express (and I'm a writer, so that's saying something).

Dad—you are and always will be my hero. Thank you for teaching me how to stand tall and keep pushing forward, even when the words won't come.

To my brothers, Mike and Bill—Mike, you make me feel like I can wrestle a grizzly (or at least a rough draft). Bill, your music reminds me that creativity doesn't come with conditions or deadlines—just truth.

Larry Brown—your guidance during the hardest chapters of my life kept me going and growing. I wouldn't be here without you.

Winston Churchill—always by my side, you truly are man's best friend.

Scott A. Johnson—literally taught me how to write. If this book makes sense, blame Scott.

Michael Knost—thank you for helping me become a better writer and reminding me to write for me, not for the algorithm.

Gareth Jones—you pulled me out of my comfort zone and into a higher gear. You didn't just coach me on my writing; you helped me upgrade my voice.

Rebecca Cuthbert—you saw something worth publishing in my scribbles. That alone is proof that editors have superpowers.

D.L. Winchester—thank you for editing my chaos into something a reader could actually finish. You have the patience of a saint and the precision of a scalpel.

Nick Thacker—you reminded me that persistence is the name of the game. Your example keeps me showing up to the keyboard.

Heidi Ruby Miller—you opened my eyes to the business side of writing and taught me how to start building my network.

And finally, to A.G. Riddle—your novels were my gateway drug. They sparked the fire and made me believe storytelling was not just possible, but necessary.

To all of you: I may have written this book, but you helped build it. Thank you from the bottom of my ink-stained heart.

If you are a fan of horror stories and tales,
you'll want to follow Undertaker Books.
We're bringing you stories to take to your grave.

www.ingramcontent.com/pod-product-compliance
Lightning Source LLC
Chambersburg PA
CBHW060315310726

48976CB00007B/2340